The Making of Herman Faust

MICHELE E. GWYNN

An M.E. Gwynn Publication

Cover by Emeegee Graphics

Editing: M.E. Gwynn

The Making of Herman Faust is an M.E. Gwynn Publication.

Contents

V

1. Chapter 1 1
2. Chapter 2 11
3. Chapter 3 19
4. Chapter 4 35
5. Chapter 5 43
6. Chapter 6 53
7. Chapter 7 65
8. Chapter 8 83
9. Chapter 9 93
10. Chapter 10 109
11. Chapter 11 121
12. Chapter 12 127

Also By Michele E. Gwynn 143

When the walls come tumbling down...

Herman Faust is the no-nonsense Direktor of the LKA (The LandesKriminalamt, similar to the American CIA) and long-time friend of Kommissar Joseph Heinz. His career spans thirty years, and he is now on the cusp of retirement. Although usually cool and in control it wasn't always so for Faust. With experience, came wisdom, hard won wisdom for which he paid a high price.

1988: For rookie officer Herman Faust, a routine, late night traffic stop turns into the apprehension of a high priority defector, one with ties to the Soviet bio-weapons program Obolensk. After bringing the woman and her brother in for questioning, the man disappears, and the woman is found inside her holding cell...dead. The American CIA intervenes, confiscating the woman's corpse and demanding answers even as more bodies pile up around them. Faust has none to offer, but begins receiving anonymous calls threatening his family, and his own life. As clues come to light linking his superior, Captain Rolf Rheinhardt, to the woman, and to a Soviet plot to launch a biological weapon on the American Embassy, Faust knows he must risk all to stop the deadly pathogen from being released on innocent civilians. The stability of West Berlin is at risk, and if Faust fails to solve the case, it will be war! This is his story. This is the making of Herman Faust.

Chapter One

"Please, get out of the car." The request was issued with authority.

Inside the sedan, a man with dark hair and a slight build began to exit the driver's side door. He pulled his coat tighter around him while shifting his eyes left and right.

"I really don't see why this is necessary..." he began. "I have my papers here." He reached inside his coat.

"Stop!" The blond officer pulled his service revolver out, aiming it dead center of the man's chest. "Raise your hands and turn around! Place them on the roof of your vehicle, and do not move!"

He approached the man, placing the gun at his back. With one hand, the officer reached around, patting him down first on one side, then the other. Finally, he retrieved the papers found inside the gentleman's coat. He stepped back, and attempted to read them, but it was dark on the side of the road, and rain fell in a soaking mist.

The man glanced over his shoulder. "I'm Gunter Meyer. A banker. I live at Number 52, Kreutznacherstrasse in Steglitz."

The officer nodded, muttering, "Figures. Jewish, and a banker." He handed the papers back. "You may turn around."

Gunter Meyer turned slowly as he put his papers back into his coat pocket.

"What are you doing out so late, and so close to the border of the DDR?"

Meyer shifted his weight. "I was merely out for a drive. Is that now against the law too?"

The blond officer remained quiet, staring at Meyer. He still held the gun in his hand, and it was still aimed in the man's direction.

Meyer cast his eyes down, and then back up. "Well? Can I go or am I being detained?"

"Is there a reason I should detain you?"

"What? No! Of course not. I was simply asking..." Meyer huffed. He clenched and unclenched his hands, a clear sign of his anxiety.

The officer shrugged. "You may go, but I would not make a habit of these moonlight drives. It's not safe out here." He began to holster his firearm.

Meyer's frame lost some of its rigidity. He turned, ducking into the driver's seat, relieved. A muffled sneeze broke the silence. Meyer froze, and then reached to slam the door shut while trying to start the car.

The officer cursed, pulled his gun once again, and aimed it precisely at Meyer's head. "Stop! I will shoot!"

Meyer was caught between his panic to flee, and the inner voice shouting at him to stay still, don't do anything to cause the officer to pull that trigger.

"Keep your hands where I can see them! Slowly exit the vehicle, and lay down on the ground, face first!"

The banker hesitated.

"Now!"

Defeat filled Meyer's large, dark eyes. He lifted both hands, moving at a pace he hoped would not antagonize the police officer. "Please, just please be calm."

"Shut up! Get down!" The officer came around to Meyer's side, and when he'd fully complied, quickly handcuffed the man. Meyer lay on the road unable to rise. "Stay there, or by God, I will shoot you like a dog!"

The officer searched the car. The sedan had a small backseat, barely any room for a person to sit comfortably, and no one was sitting there. The officer then pushed and prodded the cushions. At the last tug, the entire back seat popped up revealing a hidden nook.

Lying inside the hollowed-out space was a woman. She appeared to be in her early thirties with long, dark hair, and large brown eyes. She blinked at the German officer staring down at her.

"Please," came Meyer's plea. "She's my sister. Don't hurt her."

The officer huffed. He'd seen this a dozen times already. Since his first few days out of the academy, he'd witnessed people being smuggled out of East Germany. He didn't even know how they managed it since the guards inside the DDR were not only thorough, but brutal if they came across anyone trying to escape. Most of those who attempted it ended up shot right where they stood. Those that weren't killed on the spot wished they had been by the time the Stasi were finished with them. But the ones who made it never expected kindness from the police. It was foreign to them.

"I'm not going to hurt her, you fool. I'm not the Stasi. This isn't East Germany." He turned back to the woman and extended his hand. "You can come out."

She took his hand with some hesitation, carefully climbing out of the hidden well beneath the bench seat. When she stood on the pavement, he holstered his gun, and introduced himself.

"I'm Officer Herman Faust. Welcome to West Germany, Miss?"

"Edith Meyer Hoffmann." She gave her full name.

"And where is Herr Hoffmann?" Faust inquired after her husband. "Is he somewhere in the car too?" He lifted one thick eyebrow.

Her expression fell. "No. He's dead. Shot down not two hours ago." Tears welled in her eyes and began to fall down her gaunt cheeks.

"Edith..." Meyer's voice tried to offer comfort.

Faust sighed. "I'm sorry, Frau Hoffmann. You have my condolences." He turned to Meyer, bending down to release him from the cuffs. "No funny business from you, Meyer." Faust unlocked the wrist cuffs, and stood, reaching a hand out to help the man up. "You both will, of course, need to come down to the station to give a statement."

"Is that really necessary?" Meyer looked at his sister who was shaking visibly with grief.

"I'm afraid so. Come. You'll ride with me. I'll send someone to pick up your car and bring it to the station house."

Faust guided them to his own vehicle. Frau Hoffmann slid into the back seat of the police cruiser. Her brother reluctantly climbed in beside her.

"Will this take long?" Meyer asked. "My sister is not well."

Edith Hoffmann patted her brother's arm, a wan smile on her lips. "I'll be okay, Gunter." She coughed.

Faust looked in the rearview mirror. "It will take as long as it takes, I'm afraid, but we will be sure to bring in a physician if that is what she requires."

"That won't be necessary, officer," she said, looking out the window into the dark of night.

"Edith—"

"I'll be all right. Just let's get on with this. We're safe now, brother. We're safe." She spoke softly, seeming unconcerned.

Faust heard the resignation in her voice, and the relief. Even if her brother didn't realize it yet, Edith Meyer Hoffmann was correct. They were, indeed, safe now.

He cranked the ignition and pulled onto the road. The ride back to the station was slow-going as the rain began to fall in sheets. With the December temperatures dropping below freezing overnight, there would be nothing but ice covering the roads by morning. Herman was glad he'd remembered to put the chains on the tires. His wife, Helga, would need the traction to make it into work. He would be getting off shift only an hour before, just in time to make it home to take care of Therese, their daughter. At three, she was the apple of his eye, and had her papa wrapped around her dainty finger. Still, she was a handful, especially when he had to work overnight. At least his mother-in-law, Margaret, would arrive in the morning to watch the tike while he got some sleep.

Margaret stayed until Helga came home, and by then, Herman was getting up for his next shift. It wasn't an easy schedule, but it worked for them, for now.

Before he knew it, they'd arrived at the station. Faust pulled into the parking lot and found a spot. He had no umbrella on hand, but he did carry an extra jacket. He handed it to Frau Hoffmann after opening the back door to let her and her brother out.

"Here," he said, throwing the coat over her shoulders, and flipping the hood up, "this should help keep you dry."

Meyer exited the vehicle, and they ran for the front door. Inside, the station house was quiet. Faust took Meyer and his sister to in-processing. He left them both in the desk Sergeant's hands while he reported in to his Captain.

"Another made it across. She's in with Herring right now."

Captain Rolf Rheinhardt looked up, his keen green eyes locking with Faust's as his dark eyebrows lowered. "She?"

"Yes, a widow. Recent widow. Her husband did not make it."

"I see. She had help?"

Faust nodded. "Yes, her brother. He's one of ours, a Jewish banker."

Rheinhardt grunted. "Have you run his background check yet?"

"Nein. I'm on my way to my desk now. I'll run it and fill out my report."

The captain nodded, dismissing Faust who turned to leave.

"Faust?"

Herman paused, looking back.

"What's her name?"

"Hoffmann. Edith Meyer Hoffmann. The brother is Gunter Meyer."

Rheinhardt froze. "And her husband?"

Faust returned to the doorway. "Herr Hoffmann?" he offered.

The captain rummaged through his desk, locating a file folder. He pulled it out, flipping through the pages. Finally, he stopped, and pointed at the two pictures on the page. "Is this her?" He turned the folder toward Faust.

Hermann approached, looking down. On the page were two faded photographs. One was of a tall, good-looking man with prominent cheekbones and a thin mustache. He wore wire-rimmed glasses over his blue eyes and was dressed in a dark suit. The other picture showed a young woman with long, dark hair and creamy cheeks, smiling, wearing a wedding gown. She was the picture of health and happiness holding a modest bouquet of white roses. Despite the difference in age and obvious declining health now, there was no doubt this was a picture of Edith Meyer on her wedding day.

"Yes, that's her. Why? Who is she?"

Rheinhardt ran a hand over his mouth. "She is the wife of one of the top microbiologists in the world. Solomon Hoffmann. Back in the early '70s, Hoffmann was caught on the wrong side of the wall while on a special dispensation to visit his dying grandmother. He was recruited by

Vector to help develop biological weapons for the Soviets. Since then, we've lost track, but he more than likely moved on from Vector to Obolensk, the newest branch of their germ warfare division. You said he didn't make it?" He looked at Faust.

"Frau Hoffmann said he died not more than two hours before I came upon them. What does this mean?"

"I don't exactly know yet, but now we have her. She was his wife. She'll have information." He picked up the phone.

"Who are you calling?" Faust asked. His captain seemed agitated, a clear shift from his usually calm demeanor.

Rheinhardt chewed his lip. "The Landeskriminalamt will want her." Dialing, he glanced over his shoulder. "Good work, Faust. Now, go write that report."

Chapter Two

An hour later, Faust finished his report and dropped it into the inbox on his Captain's desk to be signed off. Rheinhardt was away from the office. Faust sighed, knowing he would need to return to patrol now that his paperwork was completed. He thought about what his Captain said. Frau Hoffmann's husband was apparently a high priority acquisition for the west. In Hoffmann's absence, his wife became second prize. After all, as his spouse, she would most likely have knowledge of his work, might even be in possession of his research—whatever it happened to be—although Faust had not searched her person himself. She wasn't a criminal. Her lack of criminal status, and her non-threatening appearance had made him complacent, allowing her to escape a pat down. Still, he was curious if Sergeant Herring had discovered anything.

He decided to stop by the holding cells on his way out. It wasn't often something this intriguing occurred.

It was quiet save for the sound of rain slapping the tin roof of the small station house. Herring was nowhere to be found. Faust sniffed, raising an eyebrow as he bypassed the Sergeant's desk and headed back toward the holding cells. He felt all alone in the world in this moment, what with no one about. It appeared the night shift had it easier than the daytime crew, at least, the ones who weren't assigned to patrol. Faust entered the back rooms and came to the secured door that led to the cells. He punched in the authorization code and waited as the light on the lock turned green, buzzing. The loud sound pierced the silence. He turned the knob and entered.

Inside, there were six independent cells, all 4 x 8 feet in size. Just enough room for a cot, a toilet, and a sink. Each also contained a small window approximately 12 inches wide and 18 inches long. The glass was unbreakable, but at least it allowed for the smallest of views outside. The grayish-green paint on the concrete walls showed its age as it cracked and peeled, revealing an old building and its lack of funding.

He didn't know which cell she was in, so began peering through the small windows of each door. The first three cells were empty. The next contained a gray-haired man loudly snoring off a beer-bender. The fifth cell was also empty leaving the last cell on the left the only likely spot where Frau Hoffmann would be held. Faust peeked into the window, speaking before laying eyes upon her.

"Are you okay in there, Frau...?" The words died on his lips.

Edith Meyer Hoffmann's body was sprawled across the cold concrete floor. Blood oozed from her nose, lips, and one exposed ear.

"Guard!" Faust shouted, running back to the security box by the main entry to punch in the code that would open that door. "Guard!" He yelled again, throwing the steel door wide.

Herring came running from the bathroom, tucking his shirt in. "What is it, Faust?"

"Frau Hoffmann, she's unconscious on the floor! Call an ambulance!" He ran back in, punching another code. The door to cell six slid open. Herman Faust ran inside, dropping to his knees beside the woman.

"Frau Hoffman," he pushed two fingers against her carotid artery, feeling for a pulse. "Edith! Can you hear me?" With no pulse found, he straightened her neck and leaned down, turning his ear toward her nose and mouth.

There was no breath. Not waiting one minute more, Faust began chest compressions.

"Well?" Sergeant Herring stood in the doorway, another officer behind him peeking, wide-eyed, over his shoulder.

"No pulse, not breathing. Did you call for help?" Faust continued depressions.

Herring turned to the lackey behind him. "Call the ambulance! Schnell!"

"Get over here, Herring, and do the breaths. Hurry!" Faust directed the Sergeant in CPR, telling him to check for any obstruction in her airway. "Pinch her nose and blow in two breaths."

Herring wiped the excess blood from her mouth and did as bid. Faust began counting out compressions once again. "Where the hell is the Captain? We need to inform her brother. She may have a medical condition we don't know about. He's here still, yes?"

Herring blinked, clearly rattled by the situation. "No. Rheinhardt took him out of here about an hour ago."

"What, why?" Faust pointed, and Herring blew in two more breaths.

The sergeant sat back up. "I don't know. He didn't say. I figured he was taking him home. We didn't have any reason to hold him."

"Shit! A fine time to take off." Faust and Herring kept up the life-saving measures until the emergency medical responders arrived. One short man in his late thirties, and a tall, young woman who looked fresh out of school took over, checking again for a pulse.

The young woman opened Frau Hoffmann's shirt, pushed her bra straps out of the way, and grabbed a defibrillator. Lifting the paddles, she said, "Clear!" before shocking Hoffmann's heart. The machine continued its monotone. She increased the amplitude and repeated the task. Still nothing. The man filled a syringe and injected the intravenous line he'd only just inserted. Once complete, the woman, again, tried to shock Frau Hoffmann's heart back to life. The monotone stretched out like a siren in the silence, never once breaking off into a steady beat.

"I'll need to inform her brother. Which hospital will you be taking her to?" Faust stood back, looking at the techs.

The short EMS technician sat back on his heels. "Whichever one has an open morgue." His partner, the tall, young woman, set the paddles back on the defibrillator, and pulled out a sheet from her bag. She shook it out and laid it over the body of Edith Meyer Hoffmann.

"What? Why did you stop?" Faust looked down at them, eyes wide and filled with shock.

"She's gone, officer. I'm sorry, but it took us more than thirty minutes to get here, and despite all your efforts, and ours, we've been unable to revive her. She's been down too long. She's gone."

Herman Faust stood, unsure what to do next. This was his first death on the job. He ran his hand over his face, chewing the inside of his cheek—a nervous habit that helped him think. His wife, Helga, often joked he would one day chew a hole right through his face.

"I need to contact the captain. If he's still with Herr Meyer..." Faust walked out of the cell and left the block. Herring followed.

"I can't believe it. She was fine when I put her in there. Maybe a little cough, and she looked rather thin, but otherwise, she seemed okay. Normal for those from the other side of the wall. And what do you think was with all that blood coming out of her nose and ears?"

"Maybe a brain hemorrhage? I don't know, Herring. That's for the coroner to figure out now."

Herring went behind his desk, wiping blood off his hands and chin with a towel. "Well, at least you didn't get blood all over you." He picked up the phone. "I'll call the captain. As soon as I get him on the line, I'll transfer him to your desk."

Faust stood, unsure of his next step. "Okay. I guess I'll be at my desk." He wandered off to his area in the back corner of the quadrant.

He sat down, stunned. Only once before had he been involved in a life-or-death situation, a choking. A perp he'd picked up for drug possession had tried to swallow the bag of drugs he carried. The bag got stuck, and the fool began to choke. Faust had immediately grabbed him around the waist, applying pressure just below the breastbone. The Heimlich maneuver was successful. The baggie of drugs was expelled, and the dealer went to jail. Alive. But this was his first death. The silence in the station house was briefly interrupted by the paramedics wheeling the body out to the ambulance. He couldn't see her face, but Edith Meyer Hoffmann was there, under the white sheet, dead.

The junior officer followed, a Polaroid camera in hand. He'd been taking pictures before the body was removed. Standard procedure. There was also closed-circuit footage inside the holding area. All of it would be collected as part of the evidence to close her case. A woman who'd escaped communist rule only to be jailed in the west, dies alone inside a cell. It was a fucking tragedy. Such shouldn't happen to anyone in Faust's opinion.

He realized he'd been sitting there for quite some time, and still, the phone hadn't rung. He looked up, seeking out Herring. The man was leaning over the front desk, rubbing his temples.

"Hey, Herring. Any luck yet?"

Herring straightened. "No, not yet."

"Keep trying." Faust sat forward. The clock on the wall showed it was 0437. His shift would end in less than three hours. There was still much to do, beginning with informing her family, which they were trying to do with zero success.

"Where are you, captain?" he muttered under his breath. No longer capable of sitting still, Herman Faust pulled out the requisite forms for an inmate death and began filling them out.

Chapter Three

Morning shift change arrived with still no word from Captain Rheinhardt. Faust walked to the front desk; his jacket slung over one arm.

"I've put all the paperwork on the captain's desk. Where on earth do you think he is? Why isn't he answering his pages?"

Sergeant Herring looked up, appearing worse for wear, shaking his head. "I don't know, Faust. Maybe he just went home after dropping Meyer off. We're all exhausted, and something seems to be going around." He coughed. "He's probably home and in bed, which is where I'm going, and you should too. We've done all we can. The rest is up to the captain when he comes in tonight."

"I suppose you're right. I have everything in my report. If he has any questions, he knows where to find me. Goodnight, Herring."

"Yeah, you too, Herman."

Faust punched out on the clock and left the station house. Outside, the morning was crisp and cold. The ground was covered in wet snow, and at least six inches of it covered his police cruiser. He sighed. He didn't feel like cleaning off a windshield, but it was necessary if he wanted to get home. He pulled on his coat, yanked his hat down over his head, and resigned himself to the task. By the time he was finished, the inside of the car had heated up.

He was grateful once he slid in behind the wheel and closed the door. His fingers felt numb, and his body ached in unusual places. His neck and shoulders screamed in pain, most likely from giving CPR for half an hour. He was tired and looking forward to getting home. More so, he was looking forward to his mother-in-law's arrival because then he could crawl into his warm bed and sleep off this hellish night.

Helga was in the kitchen when he arrived. She stood by the stove cooking eggs. He noticed she was already dressed for work, looking very professional in her suit dress. His wife was a legal secretary and knew as much about the law as her employer. She was an intelligent woman with a sparkling wit. It didn't hurt that she was also beautiful with flowing red hair and crystal blue eyes. How she chose him over all the men vying for her attention that day still stymied him, but he was grateful. He would have fought them all to win her, but as luck would have it, she was the one who threw the winning punch. He knew it was that act which won his heart.

It all went down after he'd graduated from the police academy. He and his best friend, Joseph Heinz, had gone out to celebrate, dragging along their friend, Karl Keller. Keller and Faust often argued, always on the opposite side of every issue, while Joseph seemed to be the linchpin that held their trio together. Even so, they were never far from each other's company. That evening, they made the rounds of the local pubs, feeling jovial and optimistic about their futures. Around about the third establishment, they stumbled upon a spot with a good band playing lively music. It was there that they all spotted her, a gorgeous girl with flaming hair sitting with her friends.

Herman smiled at her, unable to help himself, and she smiled back.

Joseph whistled, saying, "Now there's a looker, Herman!"

"That she is, my friend, and I do believe she's looking at me so roll your tongue back up into your mouth." Faust laughed as he patted Joseph on the shoulder.

Karl smirked. "That wasn't you she was smiling at, Faust, it was me! That one there is all mine."

Herman's eyebrows lowered. "Want to bet on it?"

Joseph noticed the serious turn his friend's mood had taken and tried smothering his own grin even as his brows rose in surprise. "Gentlemen, I do believe we have a wager. May the best man win?"

"You stay out of it, Joseph!" Faust grunted, unaware that his best friend was already backing off from participating in the bet even as he kept quiet, silently laughing. But Karl Keller did not back off. Before Joseph could reel the man in, Keller had boldly walked up to the red-haired beauty and asked her to dance. She'd glanced over in Herman and Joseph's direction before politely agreeing. As the band played, Keller spun the lovely girl around the dance floor while Herman fumed.

When the song ended, Keller tried to pull her along for another dance. Joseph appeared behind them. "May I cut in?"

The girl eyed Joseph, and seeing her chance to escape, accepted. "Of course." Keller had no choice but to relinquish her hand. He wandered over to the edge of the floor and watched, impatient.

Joseph looked down at her as he led her through the polka. "I hope I wasn't intruding..." He left the statement hanging.

"Not at all."

"I'm Joseph," he said. Heinz glanced over at Herman who stood, hands in pockets, glaring at him. Heinz chuckled. "And that one over there is Herman, my best friend."

"He looks quite put out," she said.

"Yes, well, he wanted to dance with you, but Karl beat him to it."

"He did?" She turned her large, lovely blue eyes on him.

"Oh, yes. That's why he's glaring at me now. Thinks I'm stepping on his toes." The grin spread across his face.

"And are you?" She offered an inquiring look.

Joseph noticed the laughter in her eyes and, caught off guard by both her boldness and her beauty, stumbled. He righted them both immediately. "No, but it does seem I'm stepping on yours. Sorry!"

She laughed. "I'm Helga, by the way."

"It's nice to meet you, Helga. There's not a boyfriend somewhere around here, is there?"

"You sure do ask a lot of questions."

"I'm practicing."

"For what?" she said.

"Well, we've just graduated from the police academy. We're officially police officers. One day, I hope to be a detective. Herman, too. He's very smart, that one. Don't let his silly hair fool you."

She looked at the man in question. His blond hair fell in a wave over his eyes, refusing to stay slicked back. "I don't think his hair is silly. In fact, it's quite nice."

The song ended, and Joseph offered his arm, intending to lead Helga to Herman, and let them take it from there. Karl reappeared, grabbing Helga's hand.

"Another go-round, sweets?" He leaned in, trying to kiss her.

Helga recoiled in horror, balled up her fist, and smacked Karl hard across the jaw. The young man stumbled backwards and landed on his ass. Joseph stood with his mouth hanging open in shock. From twenty feet away, Faust came running.

"Are you alright?" he asked her, concern in his voice. "You didn't hurt your hand, did you? Christ, let me see your knuckles?" He took her hand, holding it gently, examining each finger.

"It's fine. I'm fine. Thank you." Helga blushed. Unsure what to say, she could only stand still, allowing Faust to continue holding her hand.

As they stared at each other, Joseph smirked and backed away. Karl tried to rise, anger blazing in his eyes as he looked at Herman holding the girl's hand. Joseph stepped in quickly, pulling Karl away. A waltz struck up, and Herman and Helga drew closer, slowly melding together as they began to dance, unaware that a roomful of people watched them, their attention drawn to the feisty redhead who'd just clobbered one man, and now seemed to be calmly enjoying the company of another.

They'd been together ever since. It was on the day of his wedding when Faust finally thought to ask Joseph exactly what he'd said to Helga that first night. Discovering the truth, he felt like a complete ass for thinking his best friend had tried to horn in on his love. It had, in fact, been the opposite. Joseph set them up. For that, he was eternally grateful.

Now, Helga stood before him, a welcome sight, especially after last night. She turned, smiling, as she flipped the eggs over in the pan.

"Good morning, dearest. How was your night?"

Faust slipped off his coat, hung it on the back of the kitchen chair, and walked to her. Without a word, he took her in his arms, and held her, burying his face in her hair. Silently, Helga slipped her arms around his waist, and allowed herself to be held. They stood that way for a long minute, just the two of them, no words spoken.

"Smart lady," he kissed the top of her head, "you always know exactly what I need."

Helga smiled softly into his shoulder. "Well, of course." She turned her face up to him, kissing his lips briefly. "Bad shift?"

"The worst. A lady died." He told her what he knew.

"That's terrible, Herman. And no word from your captain?"

"None. I left him a detailed report. I suppose I'll know more tonight. Right now, I'm just exhausted."

"Well, mother should be here in a few minutes, and Therese will be taken care of, so just go to bed. Get some sleep. It will all be okay, love."

On cue, Therese toddled into the kitchen. "Papa!" She flung herself at his legs, holding them tight.

Faust looked down at her long red curls and felt love swell in his heart. "Yes, munchkin, it's your papa. I'm home." He released his wife to bend down and pick up his daughter. "Guten morgen, Liebling. Did you sleep well?"

Therese placed her hands on either side of her father's face, and leaned in, touching her nose to his. "Yes!"

"That's good. Did you remember to sleep a little for your dear papa too?"

"I can't sleep for you too," the child giggled.

"Well, no wonder I'm so tired then, greedy girl."

"Go, sit," Helga directed them. "Breakfast is ready."

Faust carried his daughter to the kitchen table where he sat her down in her highchair, and then took his own seat. Helga plated their eggs and ham slices, taking the time to cut Therese's ham into small bite sizes. Together, they sat eating, enjoying the moment.

Hearing a car pulling into the driveway, Helga announced, "Mom is here, and it's time for me to leave." She rose, kissing Therese on her head, and paused to look at Herman.

"I'm okay," he said. "Go. I'll get some sleep and see you before I leave for shift." He stood, carrying his plate to the sink.

"You're sure?"

He turned. "Yes. I'm sure. But I love that you asked."

"Well, I love you, you fool." Helga embraced her husband, resting her chin on his chest as she stared up into his eyes."

Faust smiled. "So that's why you married me?" He chuckled, kissing her lips softly.

"That, and you're very cute." With one last kiss, Helga pulled away just as her mother came in the side door of their small home.

"It's bad out there. Herman, you put the chains on Helga's tires?" Margaret shook off her coat, stomping the snow off her feet in the mudroom.

He looked at his mother-in-law. "Yes, Mutti."

"For once I didn't need to remind you," she said, walking into the kitchen. Her eyes lit upon her granddaughter. "Hello, sunshine!"

"Oma!" Therese grinned, holding her arms out to her grandmother.

Faust shook his head and glanced at Helga, who shrugged. "Thank you, mother. There's soup in the refrigerator for lunch and rolls in the breadbox."

"Go. I got this. You think I don't know how to take care of a child? How do you think you grew up?" Margaret shooed her daughter out the door. "And you," she addressed Herman, "can go to bed. You look like you're going to fall asleep on your feet."

"I feel like it." Faust ruffled his daughter's hair, passing by. "Don't let her drive you crazy."

"She won't. Old Herr Duncan is out shoveling the sidewalk. Maybe we can play outside a little later. It should warm up enough to let her burn off some energy."

"Shout if you need anything." He walked around the corner and headed to bed, hoping sleep would wipe the image of the dead woman from his mind, and that when he awoke, he would get some answers from his captain.

Sleep did not come easy. First, it was a nightmare revolving on a loop inside his head. Gunter Meyer and his sister, Edith Meyer Hoffmann, were both stuffed inside the hidden space beneath the man's backseat, which didn't make sense. Then a phone rang, and Captain Rheinhardt reminded him that the LKA wanted to brief the scientist and her brother immediately. He shouted at Faust to quickly remove the two from the car and bring them in. When he tried to comply, Meyer was missing, and Edith was dead. Her blood covered the car, and behind him, a unit of men wearing HazMat suits told him to back away with his hands up. Faust awoke around three in the afternoon, covered in a cold sweat. His mouth was dry, and his head ached. He needed water and some aspirin. Herman rose to make his way to the kitchen. He found his mother-in-law packing ice into a towel, and his daughter sitting on the edge of the table crying.

"What happened?" He moved quickly to Therese's side.

"She fell off her tricycle. She's okay. It's just a small bump, but I'm putting some ice on it anyway." She came back with the cold compress.

"Give it to me," Faust barked as he grabbed it from her, placing it on the bump growing red and angry on his daughter's forehead near her temple. "How did this happen?" He scooped the small child up, cradling her as he held the ice pack in place with his free hand, all the while whispering assurances to her. "It's okay, Liebling. Daddy has you. No worries, okay?"

"It hurts," she cried.

"I know. I know, but it will stop in a minute. Be calm." He paced, gently rocking her, and looked at Margaret. "Well?"

Margaret's eyes reflected the anguish she attempted to conceal. She did not like seeing her granddaughter in tears. "We were going up and down the sidewalk on her bike.

There was a patch of ice, I think, and her foot slipped off the pedal. She toppled right over and banged her head. Not too hard, but enough to give her a good bump. For a moment, she just lay there, unmoving." A shadow passed through Margaret's blue eyes. "Then she cried out, and I knew she'd only hurt herself. I picked her up and brought her inside. That's when you came in."

He felt instantly guilty for sniping at her. She loved Therese every bit as much as he did, and he knew she hadn't done anything wrong. It was an accident. That was all.

"Okay."

He looked down at his child whose cries had already subsided into sniffles. She seemed alright. She was a tough little munchkin, and God knew he'd survived far worse scrapes as a child than this. His heartbeat was returning to normal, and the ice pack seemed to be doing its job. The bump appeared less angry, less red. In a little while, it would be nothing more than a small bruise, which they would still have to explain to Helga when she came home.

"Do you think we should take her to the clinic and let them check her out?" Margaret asked, still worried.

"No. Not unless anything else develops. Let's just keep her calm and awake for the next hour and see how she's doing then. If she gets a headache or nausea, I'll take her in, but otherwise, I think she'll be okay."

"Alright then. Can I help? You were up. Did you need something?"

"I was after a glass of water and some aspirin."

"I'll get that for you." She went to the counter, grabbing a glass and filling it before finding some aspirin in the medicine cabinet. "Here." She handed over two small, white pills.

Herman sat down, holding Therese with one arm, balancing the makeshift ice pack on her head while he popped the pills and swallowed them down with a swig of water.

"You're sick, Papa?" Therese asked.

He smiled. "You've given me your headache, which means your head should be feeling pretty good now. Does it?"

She grinned. "You can't take my headaches."

"What? Of course I can. I'm your papa, and I have magical powers." He waved his free hand over her face like a magician. "Alacazam!" He snapped his fingers. "See? I bet your head doesn't hurt, does it?"

"You're silly, papa," she giggled.

"Silly and magical."

Herman sat entertaining Therese while Margaret set about preparing dinner. It wasn't part of her usual babysitting duties, but guilt drove her to it. Clearly an act of desperation so Helga would not be quite so distraught once she learned that Therese had been injured on her watch, not that she would blame her. But that didn't matter because Margaret blamed herself. By the time Helga arrived, a little more than an hour had passed, and Therese was feeling better. In light of her recovery, Helga wasn't quite as upset as everyone thought she would be. Faust, on the other hand, was dog-tired after very little sleep. He ate dinner, and then prepared for another long, cold night, hopefully one that at least provided some answers if nothing else. He prayed that his shift would be uneventful, a prayer that, as the evening progressed, went unanswered.

Chapter Four

The station house was in a state of chaos. Captain Rheinhardt was missing. No one had seen or heard from him, least of all, the dayshift captain, Maximilian Schneider, who remained to cover the night shift while launching an investigation into Rheinhardt's whereabouts. Worse, Sergeant Herring had called in sick. A junior officer was pulled off foot patrol to man the desk in his absence, leaving them short.

"Faust!" Schneider bellowed from his office as Herman passed by to clock in. "Come in here."

Herman hesitated, knowing he'd catch hell if he failed to clock in on time. "Sir," he stepped inside the doorway, a questioning look on his face. "I need to punch in."

"It can wait." Schneider insisted, pointing at the chair opposite his desk.

Faust took a seat and waited to see what trouble he was in now.

The captain held a stack of papers in his hand. Herman recognized them as the report he'd written up and put on Rheinhardt's desk the night before.

"I've read your report." He sighed, clearly tired and more than a little aggravated. "Start from the beginning. I want to know who this woman was."

Faust fidgeted, clasping his hands before him. "I can only tell you what Rheinhardt told me, sir. Her name was Edith Meyer Hoffmann. She was smuggled outside of the wall somehow with the help of her brother, Gunter Meyer. It was a routine traffic stop for me until I discovered he was harboring someone inside his vehicle. I brought them in to give a statement, and Herring took them in for processing. Per our protocol, I informed the captain, and when he learned her name, he was the one who told me she was the wife of an East German scientist who works for the Soviets, in some place called Obolensk."

"It's not a place, Faust, it's the scientific arm of the Russian government for biological warfare."

"He said something similar. Anyhow, next thing I knew, the woman was dead in her holding cell, and both Rheinhardt and Meyer were gone. Herring said they'd left earlier, that the captain was taking him home."

"Didn't you think that was odd?" Schneider drilled him like a Stasi interrogator.

"Not really. I brought them in to the station. Meyer's car was left behind. I was going to send someone for it, but if the captain wanted to take him to it, or home, it wasn't my business."

Schneider stared down his nose at Faust for a long minute. "What else? Did Rheinhardt say anything else? Did he make any calls?"

Herman blinked. "Yes. At least, he was making a call before I left his office to type up the report."

"To whom?"

Faust thought back. "He commented that the LKA would want to talk to her. That's all I know."

The captain made a note. "I'll have the phone log checked."

"Sorry, sir, but any word on her brother? Did anyone inform him?"

Schneider looked up, then sat back in his chair, eyeing the young officer. "No. Gunter Meyer has not been informed."

This just seemed wrong to Herman. "I don't understand. This was his sister. He needs to know. I'll go myself if necessary. I know we're short-handed tonight—"

"He's dead, Officer Faust."

Herman paused, his mouth agape.

"Meyer's body was found earlier today floating in the Havel River five miles downstream from his home. The coroner is performing a rush autopsy, but the preliminary findings are fairly conclusive. He was shot three times in the chest. Either he died first and was thrown into the river, or he drowned as a result of his injuries. What I need is a forensics report on the bullets, and final word from Doctor Menghala. Oh, and I've sent an investigator to Sergeant Herring's home. It seems far too suspicious under the circumstances for him to be calling in sick."

"Actually, he began feeling under the weather last night, not long after the paramedics carried Frau Hoffmann's body out," said Faust.

Schneider stood, picking up his phone as he angrily punched the numbers. "And why didn't you note this in your report?"

Faust was taken aback. "It had nothing to do with the case, sir."

The captain grumbled, waiting for someone to pick up. "It's Schneider. Send a HazMat team to Sergeant Herring's home. Lock it down, quickly! He had contact with the body." He hung up and began pacing. Finally, he stepped around his desk and past Herman where he pushed the office door shut with a bang.

Faust jumped in his seat.

"Herman," Schneider began, trying for a calmer tone of voice, "there's more."

Faust looked at him, fear creeping into his blue eyes. "What is it?"

Schneider came back and sat on the edge of his desk, looking down at Faust. "The paramedic, the one who performed CPR, is also sick, getting worse by the hour."

"What? But, sir, I was the first to begin CPR on her..."

"Did you come into contact with her blood?" Schneider asked, deadly serious as he stood and backed up. "Do you feel ill?"

"No. Not at all. Well, I had a bit of a headache earlier, but I took some aspirin and it went away."

"Any coughing? Fever? Bleeding from your ears, eyes, or mouth?"

"No. None of that. I feel fine, and I didn't get any blood on myself. I did the chest compressions until the paramedics arrived. It was Herring who performed the mouth to mouth...at my direction," he said in growing horror. "Oh, dear God. Is he going to die?"

Schneider seemed only slightly relieved. "We need to get you checked out right away, Faust, just in case."

Herman gripped the arms of his chair. "But my wife, my daughter?"

"One crisis at a time. I'll send a medical team to pick them up. First, let's get you to the hospital. I'll have an ambulance come to pick you up, but in the meantime, I need you to go into a holding cell, for all our protection."

Faust stood, feeling shaky as fear seeped into his bones. Worry for his family muddled his thinking. "Okay, sure. But, how? Why? What the hell was she carrying?"

Schneider preceded him to the door, throwing it open wide and stepping out of Herman's way. "The hospital coroner. She discovered the organism in Hoffmann's blood during routine lab tests. It's a fast-acting toxin that attacks the white blood cells and breaks down the lining of healthy cells. To put it in laymen's terms, it was inserted into a virus that causes cells in the body to degrade until a person bleeds to death. The coroner is almost one hundred percent sure it only spreads through contact with the blood and body fluids, but until we know for sure it's not airborne, we need to keep you confined."

They walked down the hall and through central command to the corridor leading to the holding cells. Schneider punched in the code and allowed Faust to enter the secure area.

"Cell number six is off limits for now until we get a decontamination crew in to clean it, so I'll put you next door in five." He entered the code, and the steel door to cell number five rolled open.

Herman stood looking into the small, depressing interior, disbelief written all over his face. He looked at Captain Schneider. "Will you let me know once my wife and daughter are at the hospital?"

"Of course. You'll probably arrive at the same time."

Faust nodded, and taking a deep breath, stepped inside. The door began rolling closed immediately behind him.

Chapter Five

The examination took no more than twenty minutes. Doctor Zara Liebermann checked Faust's eyes, ears, throat, and then drew several vials of blood. She sent those off to the lab, reassuring him as she did.

"I see no signs of hemorrhaging. Your focus is clear, and you're not showing any symptoms associated." She lifted Faust's arms out. "Hold them here," she said. Doctor Liebermann let go, watching to see if either of Herman's arms suddenly fell. Neither did. "When a person has a brain hemorrhage, they exhibit symptoms of stroke. Your speech is clear, no weakness on either side. If you'd contracted this virus the coroner discovered upon contact with the deceased, you'd already be presenting with visible evidence of full infection. You were lucky, Officer Faust."

Herman sighed, then quickly looked up. "And my wife Helga? Our daughter?"

Doctor Liebermann pulled off the latex gloves, her lips pursed. She sat down on the stool, looking Faust in the eye. "Your wife is asymptomatic," she began.

Faust felt relief flood him, but it was short-lived.

"But your daughter," Liebermann shook her head, "has a high fever, and if we can't bring it down, she'll begin to have seizures. Her lab work is pending, but her symptoms do not coincide with what we currently know. Did she have any contact with you following your experience with Edith Meyer Hoffmann?"

His heart constricted. "I don't know..." he paused. "When I came home this morning, I did see her, of course." He thought back. "I remember picking her up in the kitchen. I was still in uniform, but," he shook his head, emotions tightening his throat, "I should have been more careful. I didn't think."

Liebermann patted his arm. "Don't beat yourself up. As I said, what she presents with is not at all in line with what we know of this virus. Still, she is a child, and what little we know about this might affect children in a different manner. We won't know until the report comes back from the lab. Right now, we have her in isolation, receiving fluids and antibiotics to bring down the fever and help her fight off any infection." Liebermann stood. "Truly, her condition seems more appropriate to a concussion than a virus, but—"

Faust jumped up. "She had a fall!"

"When?"

Herman ran a hand through his hair. "Sometime in the afternoon. I woke with a headache and went to the kitchen. My mother-in-law was there with Therese. They'd just come in. She said she'd fallen off her tricycle, but that it was just a bump." He looked hopeful.

The doctor nodded. "I'll let you know when her labs come back. In the meantime, I'm ordering a CAT Scan." She headed toward the door.

"Can I see my wife?"

Liebermann turned to leave. "She's in the next room. I'll send her in."

Faust paced, waiting. He didn't need to wait long. Helga ran through the door, and straight into his arms.

"Herman, what in God's name is going on?"

He held her close, breathing in her scent. "I don't exactly know yet."

"But something is wrong with Therese." Pain filled her voice.

He looked down into her blue eyes. "I know. The doctor thinks it's a concussion. She's ordering head x-rays or some such."

"A concussion? From what?" Then she remembered. "The fall off her tricycle? Oh, my God!" Tears pooled in her eyes, falling down her cheeks. "But mother said it was just a bump. Nothing at all, and Therese was fine. I saw her. She was okay. Just a little tired maybe, a little warm."

"I don't know, darling. It may have been more of a bump than we all realized. We'll just have to wait and see what this CAT Scan shows. At least it does not seem to be what affected the lady who died at the station. For that, we can be thankful."

"But her fever keeps rising. It began right before the damned police showed up at our door with an ambulance." She suddenly became angry, pounding on his chest. "Why didn't you call? I was terrified!"

Faust took the hits and pulled her in close. "I'm so sorry, Helga. I was caught off guard the minute I walked into work, and then Schneider detained me, put me in isolation in one of our cells. I couldn't call. He said he would take care of you both, make sure you were seen to. I'm so sorry." He'd never felt so helpless. They stood there, in the middle of the exam room, holding on to each other, silently praying their daughter would be alright. As the night wore on, the situation deteriorated.

News arrived with the lab and radiology results. Therese Faust was negative for the newly discovered virus, but her CAT Scan concluded severe concussion resulting in rapid brain swelling. Her little body could not fight both the swelling and the fever, and seizures began to wrack her tiny form. An intense discussion with Doctor Liebermann ensued. It ended with the decision to medically induce a comatose state which would allow the brain time to heal, and for the swelling to reduce. Herman and Helga could only watch, pain in their eyes, and fear in their hearts as their daughter was hooked up to a multitude of monitors and IVs.

At 7:00 a.m., a tall man with dark hair and eyes walked down the hallway and entered the ICU. His brow was set in a deep furrow as he eyed the staff coming and going, hands full of IV bags, medication, and charts. He unbuttoned his overcoat and leaned over the nurse's desk.

"I'm looking for Faust. Herman Faust. His daughter is a patient—"

"Joseph." Faust exited his daughter's room three doors down from the nursing station.

The dark-haired man turned, recognizing the voice. "Herman," he quickly thanked the nurse, and met Faust halfway. They stood facing each other, one deeply concerned, and the other, barely holding it together. "What's the news?"

Faust rubbed his face, exhaustion in the gesture. "I'm so sorry to have called you so early..."

"Don't worry about that. What can I do? How can I help?"

Faust sighed as he looked at his friend, Joseph Heinz. Moisture welled in his blue eyes as he noted the sincerity in Heinz's own. As usual, his old pal was calm and collected, and ready to help. It was who Joseph was. He didn't rile easily, and his first instinct was always to listen. Then he would find a way to make the situation better. Most people who met him thought the tall, quiet man couldn't be bothered with their problems, until he turned his attention on them, focusing like a laser. Joseph had an ability to see the big picture in all things, even if he sometimes skipped over the minutia. He could connect the dots of obscure concepts in ways that made him an ideal candidate for police work. It was a direct complement to Faust's own way of laying things out step by step. He always had a plan. They'd made a great partnership while in the academy, helping each other through the stages, completing their training near the top of their class.

Faust explained all that had occurred. "Therese is in an induced coma. The doctor hopes this will help her body heal, giving it the time and rest it needs so the swelling will go down in her brain."

"I can't believe this happened from just falling off a tricycle." Joseph sighed, speaking quietly. "How long will it take?"

Faust glanced at the floor. "She doesn't know. A day, two days," he shrugged, tired. "If it goes on longer, we're looking at possible brain damage."

"My God, Herman." Heinz reached out, gripping Faust's shoulder in a reassuring squeeze.

"I know."

"But how did you and Helga get dragged here too? You mentioned something about a case," he inquired.

"Yes, yes. That's partly what I wanted to talk to you about. I need your help." Faust chewed the inside of his cheek, thinking. "Let's take this to the lounge down the hall. I promised Helga some coffee." He moved around his friend.

Joseph spun around, preparing to follow. "Of course."

He nearly bumped into Herman, who'd stopped short.

Two men in dark suits wearing overcoats stood in their path. "Officer Herman Faust?" The first man spoke, raising a graying eyebrow. His short haircut, dark-rimmed glasses, and American accent caught both Herman's and Joseph's attention.

"Yes? Who's asking?"

The man stood still, unblinking. His cohort squared his shoulders, feet apart as if preparing for battle. That man casually parted his overcoat and jacket revealing a shoulder holster beneath with a firearm a hair's breadth from his fingertips. A badge was strapped to his belt. CIA.

"I'm Special Agent Miller, and this is Special Agent Thompson. Your Captain Schneider said we'd find you here. We need to talk. I heard you mention a lounge?"

Heinz and Faust exchanged a look, one that said, *'What the hell is going on now?'* "What does the American CIA want with me?"

"Not out here, Officer Faust. And who is this?" Miller turned his attention to Heinz, assessing him.

"This is my friend and colleague, Officer Joseph Heinz."

"Schneider made no mention of him," said Thompson. He raised a black eyebrow nearly to the hairline of his crew cut.

"He works at another borough, but he is here at my request. Whatever you need to talk to me about, you can discuss in front of him." Faust asserted casual authority into his words. He didn't like the vibe he felt coming off the Americans, and he didn't want to go anywhere with them without backup. To his way of thinking, they hadn't fully proved they were who they said they were, and his captain hadn't mentioned anything about American agents to him. Not yet, anyhow.

Miller spoke after a short pause. "Alright. The lounge, let's go there." He stepped back, letting Faust lead the way. Joseph stayed at his side, a half-step back keeping his eyes on the agents, who followed.

Chapter Six

"We need to know what you found on Edith Meyer Hoffmann and her brother when you arrested them." Special Agent Miller pushed the lounge door closed behind him. Thompson took up post standing in front of it to prevent anyone from walking in. Faust and Heinz stood by a table and chairs as the two men stared them down, unblinking. It was unnerving.

"I didn't arrest them, Agent Miller," said Faust. "I pulled Gunter Meyer over because I was patrolling near the DDR border, and he happened to be driving past."

"Then why did you pull him over?"

"It was late." Sarcasm tinged Faust's words.

Miller tilted his head. "So, you had some kind of reasonable suspicion to pull the man over?"

"It's unusual for there to be traffic in the area at that time of night, yes."

"I see. You pulled Meyer over. Your report states," Miller paused as he pulled a folded piece of paper from his pocket and shook it out, "that you were going to let Mr. Meyer go when a sound alerted you to the presence of another passenger. You searched the car and found his sister, Mrs. Hoffmann, hidden beneath the backseat." The agent refolded the paper and put it back inside his pocket. "A man you pulled over on suspicion of nefarious activity is found to have been actually involved in nefarious activity, and you didn't arrest them both?"

Faust sucked in a breath, letting it out slowly as he counted to ten. Next to him, Joseph tensed, preparing to speak on his friend's behalf when Faust gripped his arm, stopping him.

"In Berlin, we do not arrest those escaping from oppressive communism. Those people have already endured hardships and punishments we cannot begin to fathom here in the west. No, sir, we welcome them. The only reason I brought them into the station was so Frau Hoffmann could make her official statement. That is our policy. We debrief, but we do not arrest."

Miller continued to stare through his horn-rimmed spectacles, his expression giving nothing away. "So, you did not interrogate her, even knowing who she was?"

"Look, he already told you—" Joseph's words flew, angry and fast.

"It's okay, Joseph." Faust held up one hand to halt his friend. "No, I did not interrogate her. Sergeant Herring took her statement, for which I'm sure you probably have a copy of that as well in your pocket, and I did not know who she was until Captain Rheinhardt pointed it out. He is the one who recognized her name. If you have any further questions about Frau Hoffmann and her brother, you should ask him or even Sergeant Herring. Both would know more than I do."

Miller and Thompson exchanged a look before Miller spoke again. "Sergeant Herring passed about an hour ago, Officer Faust, so we cannot ask him anything."

Herman felt his heart stop. His mouth opened and froze, as if unsure whether or not to speak. Heinz gripped his friend's shoulder in sympathy.

Miller continued. "And Captain Rheinhardt is missing in action. We've already been to his residence. There is no sign he's even been there in the last twenty-four hours. His neighbor states she last saw him leaving for work yesterday. He never came home. So, officer, we have a problem. The wife of a Soviet-controlled scientist escaped the DDR, entering West Berlin bringing a deadly biological contagion with her. She is dead. Her brother is dead. Two people who've had contact with her body are dead, and the only person who knew anything about who she was is missing. You brought her in, Officer Faust. You are the only living link left. Until we find your Captain Rheinhardt, you will be required to stay put. You helped bring this weapon across, and until we're satisfied that you're not complicit in this act of war, you'll be under constant surveillance. Understood?"

"Wait, what?" Faust's mouth dropped open. "Complicit in an act of war? Are you out of your mind? And you said two other people are dead," he repeated, confused. "Who else besides Sergeant Herring?"

Thompson broke his silence. "The EMS responder, the one who performed CPR."

"Christ!" Heinz replied. "Herman, you were in contact with her too." Joseph looked at him.

"Yes and no. I've already been checked. So have Helga and Therese. It seems to be transmitted through contact with blood. Not airborne as was feared."

Heinz was visibly relieved. "Thank God."

"Indeed," said Miller, "but the virus, once contracted and activated, is only one step away from becoming airborne. Apparently, there's an incubation period. Our own team discovered this not two hours ago from the samples confiscated from the hospital coroner."

Heinz thought quickly. "And what about those in the hospital and the morgue who've had contact?"

"Already seized and quarantined," said Miller, who looked at Faust, "including your doctor, I'm afraid. I'm sure another has already taken over your daughter's care. At least she's been cleared. Be thankful for that. Officer Faust, do you know of anywhere Captain Rheinhardt could be? Anyone he'd go to?"

Faust tried to think. His mind was racing ninety miles a minute and getting nowhere. "I couldn't begin to say... All I know is he seemed well-informed about Solomon Hoffmann. He knew the name and seemed quite intrigued. He said our own LKA would be very interested in speaking with her. That's it. He charged me to writing up my report."

"Did he mention any names? Call anyone?" Miller pushed.

Faust's eyes lit. "Yes. He was calling someone when I left his office. I mentioned this to Captain Schneider. He said he would have the outgoing call log checked, but that's all I know. There's nothing else."

"Okay." Miller looked at Thomson. "We need that call log." He glanced back at Faust. "We'll be in touch. Don't go anywhere, and don't speak of this to anyone." He pinned Heinz with a sharp look. "And that goes for you too, Officer Heinz." The agents turned, leaving Faust and Heinz standing in the middle of the lounge, stunned.

"Goddamn Americans!" Heinz muttered. "Don't let them intimidate you, Herman. You've done nothing wrong."

"Except help bring in a deadly contagion from the Soviets. Dammit, Joseph! I nearly got my family killed!" Knowing how close he'd brought Helga and Therese to death felt like a punch to the gut. "And Therese is not even out of the woods yet. An induced coma, Joseph, all from a small bump on the head. What the hell am I going to do?"

Heinz patted his back. "You're going to calm down, go back to your family, and then," he paused, taking a deep breath, "pray."

Faust nodded, emotions simmering beneath the surface. He drew in a steadying breath. "Yes, that's all I can do right now, it seems."

"And don't forget Helga's coffee." Heinz turned, finding a couple of Styrofoam cups and the pot of complimentary coffee offered by the hospital.

"Christ, almost forgot. Thank you, Joseph."

"Anytime." Heinz held the door open, waiting as Faust passed through. "Was there some other deadly crisis you wanted to discuss with me or was that it?"

"No, just that one," Faust grumbled. "Smartass."

With cups of hot coffee in hand, they returned to his daughter's room, preparing for a long day.

After eight hours, Faust headed home. Helga remained at the hospital insisting she not leave Therese's side in case she improved, and the new physician brought her out of her coma. The staff brought in a rollaway bed for her, and Herman promised to return with a fresh change of clothes after a few hours of sleep. For her part, Helga promised to call immediately if there was any change. His mother-in-law had apparently dropped by earlier in the day leaving a casserole in the refrigerator. Herman was too tired to eat. Instead, he grabbed a beer, popping the cap off the bottle. He downed it in a few gulps, and then ambled off to bed. He could barely keep his eyes open.

Joseph had left the hospital earlier in the afternoon to sneak in a nap before reporting in to work. Both men worked the night shift, but in light of the recent situations with the Hoffmann woman's death, his Captain's disappearance, Sergeant Herring's death, and Faust's own family emergency, he'd been given the next few nights off. Several other boroughs had volunteered officers to fill in to cover the shortfall. Herman knew it would probably be a mess by the time he got back, but at the moment, he didn't care. His bed welcomed him, and the silence of the house calmed his tattered soul. Within moments, he was sound asleep.

At 11:33 p.m., the phone rang. Faust's eyes shot open. For a moment, he was confused, unaware of where he was or the time of night. Consciousness seeped into his brain by the third ring. Helga! He rolled over, grabbing the receiver.

"Hallo. Helga? What is it? Is Therese awake?" He rubbed his eyes.

Static crackled on the line. "Nein, nor will she ever wake again if you help the American agents." A deep voice on the line warned, a voice Herman did not recognize.

"Who the hell is this?" Faust sat up, alarmed.

"That is not your concern. What is your concern is the continued well-being of your wife and child," the voice continued as if he and Herman were old friends. "She is quite lovely, your wife, as is your daughter. She is such a small thing."

Faust sucked in a breath. "What the hell do you want?" Anger shot through him and suffused his being.

"Calm yourself. What we want is simple. Do not co-operate with the American CIA, and cease searching for Captain Rheinhardt. We know they contacted you today. If you help them in any way, I'm afraid we will not be forgiving," the voice lowered, "and your family will pay the price."

Fear seized Herman's heart, constricting the muscles in his chest. He gripped the blanket on the bed, twisting it, wishing it was the neck of the coward on the other end of the line.

"Do we have an understanding, Officer Faust?" The caller waited.

Nostrils flaring, Herman nodded, and then realized he needed to speak past the lump in his throat. "We do."

"Good."

"Wait!" Herman stopped him before he could hang up.

"What is it?"

"Just what the hell are you doing? The CIA already knows about the virus. They have it contained. Whatever it is you're up to, it has already been stopped." He felt the need to push the man's buttons, to throw cold water on whatever scheme he and whoever the caller worked with had cooked up.

"Has it?" The man sounded amused. "We still have a ball in play, Officer Faust."

Seconds ticked by as Faust's mind raced.

"Rheinhardt?" Faust didn't want to believe it. His captain was an honorable man, one he was proud to be working under. Rheinhardt was a decorated officer who'd advanced to the rank of police captain in a record number of years. The man was respected by all who worked for him and with him. It was inconceivable that he might be a foreign agent.

"No more questions. Good night, officer. Remember, keep your mouth shut, and your family will remain safe." The line went dead.

Faust sat there, shaking. Whether it was fear or rage, he couldn't fathom. It felt like a mixture of both, and he didn't like it. Someone had threatened his family. Their safety was his top priority, but he'd also taken an oath to uphold the law and protect the citizens of Germany. He would not take the man's threat lying down, but first, he needed to get back to the hospital. Arrangements needed to be made to protect Therese around the clock, and Helga would need protection as well. He dialed Joseph's station asking to be patched through to his patrol car.

"Joseph, it's Herman. A situation has come up. I need your help."

For the next ten minutes, the men made plans. Afterwards, Faust collected a change of clothing for Helga, her personal items, and packed them in a bag. He changed clothes, and then armed himself with his sidearm, and two backup handguns: one at his back, and the other in his ankle holster. He'd trained for this, but it was the first time he'd carried all three on his person. There was one last thing he needed to do. Eyeing the clock on the wall, he walked to the phone, picking up the receiver, and dialed. When he was done, he placed the receiver back in its cradle, his entire body shaking from the adrenaline coursing through his veins. Faust concentrated on breathing, slowly getting himself under control. As he walked out the door, a police cruiser pulled up. Joseph sat inside waiting for him.

"Ready?" he asked, throwing open the passenger door from inside.

Faust stepped in. "Yes, let's go."

Chapter Seven

The private hospital room was more heavily guarded than the Chancellery, Berlin's answer to the White House, and ten times its size. Located in a wing utilized only for government officials and celebrities, it provided the best possible way for Faust to ensure his family's safety. He did this by calling in a favor.

"Who are these men again, Herman?" Joseph eyed the six brawny bodyguards who'd arrived on the fifth floor of the hospital. They stood in formation, like soldiers, waiting to be briefed.

"I never did fully explain about Helga's uncle, did I?" Faust glanced at the men and smirked. "Anton von Friedrich was a decorated army colonel, a former special operations expert. You know, he threatened me to within an inch of my life not five minutes before I walked out to stand at the altar to await my bride. He said if I, in any way, hurt his niece, he would, and I quote, fuck me up in ways that would make me wish I'd never been born. Then he smiled and kissed my cheeks, congratulating me. I nearly pissed myself."

"You're joking!" Heinz looked shocked. "Why didn't you ever tell me?"

"Because I was actually a little afraid of the sonofabitch. Anyhow, after Therese was born, old Uncle Anton was so happy to have another child in the family," Faust paused, and then quickly explained. "He never did have any children of his own, and he dotes on Helga. The old brute was happy for us, and after Therese's christening, he said if ever I needed anything to call on him. Well, I figured this qualified. Any threat to Helga and Therese will not be tolerated, by myself or Colonel von Friedrich."

This was stunning news. Heinz had not known this about Helga's extended family. "These men look like mercenaries."

"They are." Faust stepped forward to address them. "Gentlemen, I'm sure the colonel gave you a rundown on why you're here."

One man stepped forward. With a face carved of stone and cold eyes, he stood a head taller than Faust. His shoulders filled out his black suit jacket to capacity and then some. The hard expression in his hazel eyes could stop a bullet in its tracks and make it turn tail returning to the gun barrel from whence it fired. "I'm Major Matthias Beck, and these," he glanced back, "are my men. The colonel said his niece and grandniece are under threat by a foreign adversary. We're here to keep them safe. We will lay down our lives, if necessary," Beck's deep voice boomed.

"I hope that won't be necessary, major." Faust stood with his hands clasped behind his back. "Helga and Therese are in this room." He pointed behind him. "This is a list of hospital staff cleared to enter to attend to my daughter's care." Faust handed the major a folder containing the names of approved staff ranging from Therese's new doctor to nurses, and even one orderly. Each name listed had a background check along with a picture to identify them. "No one else goes in or out except for me and Officer Heinz." He glanced at Joseph. "I've made arrangements for meals to be brought in from the outside. Here's the vendor, his information, and a picture."

"Isn't that Jasper from The Hoffbrau?" Heinz asked, recognizing the chef from their favorite restaurant.

"It is." Faust chuckled. "Helga loves their menu, and Therese isn't eating right now. The physician has her on TPN intravenously. Until she comes out from under, that's all she gets, but when they do bring her out, I'll have Jasper bring in her favorite meal."

"Currywurst and pomme frites?" Joseph asked.

"You know it." Faust smiled.

Major Beck looked over the file, and then handed it to the mercenary behind him. The man was large, muscular, with a shaved head, and several visible tattoos on his neck. "Find a copy machine at the nurses' station and make a copy for everyone. No one comes onto this floor except those on the list. If anyone else tries, apprehend them, and bring them to me."

The man nodded, taking the file, and moving down the hall, disappearing around the corner. Beck addressed the remaining four. "You two take up post by the elevators," said Beck. "Voigt and Graf, you two take first shift guarding this door." He pointed at Therese Faust's room. "Stein and I will be here across the hall," he pointed to the empty room opposite, "and we'll relieve you at 0700. Twelve-hour shifts, gentlemen, until I inform you otherwise. Get to it." Beck returned his attention to Faust. "I expect you will keep me up to date?"

"Of course. And I'll have Jasper bring in meals for your men as well."

"That's appreciated, thank you. What else can I do to help?"

"I need as much information as possible on Captain Rolf Rheinhardt, both his service information and civilian. I cannot go through usual police channels for this right now. The captain is compromised, and I don't know how far up this goes," Faust explained.

Beck nodded. "Understood."

"I need to know who he knows, who he might be in contact with, and anything at all that might connect him to Edith Meyer Hoffmann, Solomon Hoffmann, or Gunter Meyer."

"On it. I'll contact you as soon as I find anything." Beck waited, ever the soldier, even in his current civilian state.

"Oh, sorry. Carry on, major." Faust dismissed the man, unfamiliar with being at the top of any chain of command, and yet, in this moment, he fell into the role naturally.

Heinz noticed but kept the observation to himself. "And now what do you want to do?"

Faust looked him in the eye. "Now, we go to Gunter Meyer's home, and from there, we'll search Rheinhardt's."

"Without a search warrant?" Heinz asked, surprised.

"One is dead and the other is missing. We don't have time for a warrant and notifying a judge for the need would invite too many questions, and possibly alert the one who threatened my family. Until we know what we're dealing with, we're on our own, Joseph."

"What about the Americans?"

"I don't trust them. They still haven't even explained why they're involved." Faust shook his head. "An act of war, they said. What the hell does this have to do with the American CIA anyhow? Hoffmann came here to Berlin, not to the United States. If an act of war has been committed, it's against Germany, not the U.S. No," he chewed the inside of his cheek, "no, Joseph. I don't trust them at all, and I can't involve Captain Schneider. There's no way to know who is watching me, who all the players are. If Captain Rheinhardt is involved, he has information. If he's not actively complicit, then he's being used by the Russians, which could mean he's infected, that he has been infected by them somehow, and if that's the case, we don't have a lot of time. Agent Miller said the virus hadn't fully matured, was still in some sort of incubation period, but once that passes, it will go airborne. We need to find Rheinhardt. I won't be responsible for more people dying."

"What will you tell Helga?" Heinz glanced at the door to Therese's room.

"As little as possible. I have my pager. She can contact me at any time."

Joseph nodded. "Scheisse," he mumbled, then sighed. "Well then, what are we waiting for? Let's go break into a few homes."

Herman led the way. "Indeed."

The small house in Steglitz sat at the end of a row on a corner lot. A cobblestone street ran along the northern side separating the brick Bavarian-styled cottage from the forested area growing wild on land designated as a conservation site. The lane dead-ended a half block down in a turnaround. It was the best point of entry for would-be burglars since there was no one on that side to witness such activity. Faust directed Joseph to park just off the turnaround, in the dirt, along the shoulder.

"Nice house," said Heinz. "What did he do for a living?"

"He was a banker." Faust checked his sidearm before reaching into his pocket and pulling out a rolled-up cloth.

"Figures," he replied. Faust grunted his agreement. Joseph glanced down at the cloth. "What's in there?"

Herman unrolled the beige cloth revealing small picks of various size, an old credit card, and several keys. "A lock picker's must-haves."

"And where the hell did you get those? Are you keeping something from me? A secret life as a cat burglar?"

Faust snorted. "Hardly, but in our line of work, we pick up all kinds of tips from the criminals we arrest."

"True. The best way to thwart a criminal..."

"Is to learn how to think like a criminal." Faust finished Joseph's sentence. "It's not like I'm going to be moonlighting on my off nights burglarizing homes."

"Just tonight." Joseph eyed him.

"Exactly. Just tonight, and to save lives, beginning with my own family's." Faust rolled the tools back up and shoved them into his coat pocket. Outside, the wind picked up, scattering light snowflakes on the ground. A front was moving in bringing arctic air and freezing wind chills expected by the morning.

Heinz put his car keys into his pocket, and stepped out, locking the door. The cold wind whipped his face. He pulled a knit skull cap down onto his head, covering his ears. With his dark overcoat on, no one would see the police uniform beneath. He knew he was supposed to be patrolling, but what his own captain didn't know wouldn't hurt him. He wasn't far from his zone and could keep in contact as needed via his police radio. As a precaution, he turned the volume down. The last thing either of them needed was unwanted attention.

They walked silently up the dark lane. The silence was interrupted only by the howling of the wind and rattling of the dead leaves still clinging to a few of the otherwise bare branches in the trees. It was an unsettling quiet, more so because both knew the consequences of what they were about to do, the crime they would be committing. Two police officers were about to break into the home of a dead man.

"There," Faust whispered, pointing.

Heinz looked at the first-floor window. It was located near the back of the house, facing the woods. Up close, it looked to be the window of a small study or reading room.

"Is it unlocked?" Faust asked.

Heinz gave it a tug, but it did not give.

"Let's look around back." They tip-toed through the crisp, dead grass. It was overgrown and crunched beneath their feet, sounding louder in their ears than necessary.

"There's a back door," Heinz noted. He kept to the wall, in the shadows. "Think you can pick the lock?"

Faust pulled out his tools. “I guess we’re going to find out.” He unrolled the cloth and chose one of the skeleton keys. Slipping it into the slot, he gave the doorknob a turn. Nothing. It remained locked in place.

“Here, try this one.” Heinz handed him the next of three keys. Faust tried them one by one, none of which worked.

“It would’ve been too easy, I suppose,” Faust mumbled. “Hand me the small pick and the credit card.”

Heinz complied, taking the last key, and switching it out for the requested items. “Good luck.”

Faust looked over his shoulder at Joseph, one eyebrow raised.

“What?” Heinz asked. “What am I supposed to say? Break a leg?”

A soft snort answered him. “Next you’ll be breaking out your pom poms and performing a cheer.”

“Fuck off and hurry up. It’s damned cold out here.” Heinz looked around, making sure they were still alone.

“Stop complaining, you old woman.” Faust admonished, working the pick inside the lock, and jimmying the credit card into the minuscule space between the door and the jamb. A loud click popped in the night air. Faust smiled as Joseph tensed, freezing in place. He glanced around again as Faust slowly pushed the door open.

Heinz breathed a sigh of relief. "I can't believe you actually did it."

Faust chuckled low, rising to his feet, and slipping inside. "You dared doubt me?"

Joseph followed, closing the door behind them. "Never again. Your criminal status is now sealed and forever legend as far as I'm concerned."

It was dead silent inside. A faint mustiness greeted their noses. The air had grown stale with no one there to stir it. The police had been in briefly the day before, moving items around and leaving cabinets and closets open. They would return in the oncoming days, possibly with the American CIA in tow, to tear the place apart seeking evidence of Meyer's involvement in bringing in a biological weapon. But tonight, it was just Herman and Joseph, two pawns in a deadly game of war, served cold.

"I'll take the first floor. You take the second." Faust pointed to the staircase. Heinz nodded and made his way up by the dim moonlight filtering through the window shades.

Herman walked through the kitchen, not quite knowing what he was looking for. He checked the refrigerator and the freezer. Other than a few food items, he found nothing of importance. Next, he entered the study. This was the room with the window facing the woods. It contained a solid oak desk with a leather chair that rolled around on squeaky wheels. Another tufted chair sat opposite, and a bookshelf lined one wall filled with hardback and paperback books. Some were books on banking law, both domestic and international, while others were simply old western mystery novels. It seemed that Gunter Meyer was a fan of cowboy tales.

On top of the desk sat a calendar with a date circled. It was the day he pulled Meyer over. A reminder, no doubt, of his sister's arrival, but how did she get word to him? How did Meyer know when and where to be waiting for her? Figuring there had to be some kind of letter, Faust began looking through the drawers. Other than personal tax papers and stationery, there was nothing of note.

Joseph came back down, carrying a piece of paper. "I found this in his nightstand." He handed it over.

Faust looked at it. It was a dry-cleaning receipt. "What about it?" He looked at his friend.

Heinz pointed at the top of the ticket. "Look at the address. It's located near the Checkpoint. This is the dry cleaner most of the allied soldiers use." Faust raised a questioning brow. Heinz blew out a breath. "Look on the back."

Herman flipped it over. On the backside, a number was scrawled in pencil. His eyes narrowed.

Heinz continued. "The location can't be a coincidence. What would a Jewish banker in Steglitz need with a dry cleaner so close to the Checkpoint? We should call it, see who it belongs to."

Faust folded the receipt. "No need," he said, his expression disgusted.

"What? Why not?"

"Because I already know who this number belongs to." Faust closed the desk drawer and stood.

"Who?" Heinz waited, one eyebrow raised.

Herman looked his friend in the eye. "To Captain Rheinhardt." He buttoned his coat, preparing to leave. "It's his pager number, the one we all use to contact him. The question is, what the hell was Meyer doing with it?"

"Holy hell. Now what?" Heinz followed Faust as he exited the study, making his way to the back door.

"Now, we search Rheinhardt's flat."

They left quickly, locking the back door behind them, and retracing their steps back to the car. Heinz cruised out of the neighborhood slowly, not even turning on the headlights until they cleared the block. They passed rows of parked cars tucked in for the night. One awoke with a low rumble and pulled out, merging silently into the darkness behind them.

Captain Rolf Rheinhardt lived in an apartment building on the outskirts of the Tiergarten district. They stopped once along the way to answer a page from Major Beck. Heinz kept the motor running as Herman ducked into a phone booth, dropped a coin into the slot, and dialed the number flashing on his device.

"Faust here."

"Officer," said Beck, "I have some information for you, something of note."

"On Rheinhardt?"

"Yes."

"What have you found?" Faust huddled inside the booth, his eyes sweeping the block ahead. Several cars passed, at least four. As they drove on, he relaxed.

"He was a defector."

This caught Faust by surprise. "What do you mean?"

Beck continued. "Rheinhardt came to West Berlin from the Eastern Bloc with his family when he was six years old. His mother and father brought their two children across during a brief moment when Jews were practically being expelled by the communists. His maternal grandfather, Sergei Davidovich, served in the Soviet military. He's now retired, and still living in East Berlin."

"I had no idea." Faust chewed the inside of his cheek, thinking. "Is that it?"

"No." Beck paused. "Davidovich wasn't just any soldier. He was up in rank; a Colonel-general. His name is flagged in our database, sir."

"Flagged? Spit it out, major. It's damned cold out here."

Beck cleared his throat. "The Colonel-general retired not only from the military, but as the ranking officer in charge of Obolensk. You understand the significance?" The major waited as his words sunk in.

"Scheisse!" Faust's mind raced. "But you said he's retired. Even if all the dots connect, how does that involve the captain? He was just a child then, and would likely have no contact with extended family on the other side."

Beck coughed. "No career military man is ever fully retired, Officer Faust. We all remain in the game somehow." The mercenary stated the obvious.

Faust grunted. "I see your point. Is there anything else?"

"Not at this time. I'll keep digging."

"Do that." Faust started to hang up but stopped. "Major Beck?"

"Yes?"

"Good work. Thank you." Faust hung up. The trek back to the police cruiser was a quiet one. Herman was deep in thought when a car passed as he was about to climb into the driver's seat. Heinz interrupted his solitude.

"I'm pretty sure that car has passed by here twice already." He watched as it continued slowly down the street.

"What?" Herman glanced up, eyeing the dark BMW sedan.

"It's late, and there's not much traffic out," Heinz stated. "That car has passed by now for the third time. We're being followed, Herman."

"Goddammit, by who?" Faust slammed his door shut and eyed the rearview mirror. "Pull out and go straight. Let's see what's what."

Heinz maneuvered over to the right, going straight. The car turned right ahead of them. As they passed, Faust noted the license plate. They drove down two more city blocks, and just as they passed the third side street, headlights pulled out behind them. Herman pulled down the visor and used the mirror to look back at the front of the car, but the headlights blinded his vision. He couldn't make out the front plate.

"Damn. Turn left up here," he pointed.

Heinz made the turn.

The car behind them turned left too.

"Alright, Joseph, let's see how much you learned in evading tails back in the academy." Faust slipped the seat-belt across his lap and fastened it.

"I thought you'd never ask." Joseph punched the gas pedal down, speeding up. The car behind them increased its speed. Heinz made a quick right followed by a hard left. He made it one block down, turning right again before breaking and sliding into a back alley. He shut off the engine and killed the lights. In less than thirty seconds, the other vehicle flew past them, not noticing a parked car in a side alley among several others. They could hear the brakes squealing as the tires slid on the asphalt, and then the sound of the engine speeding up again, moving away quickly. Heinz and Faust breathed a sigh of relief.

"Who do you think it was?" Heinz looked at Herman.

"I don't know. After what Beck just told me, I'm almost afraid to speculate." He scratched his head. "It's either the Americans or the bastard who called me last night. And now I'm convinced that whoever that was, is connected directly to the Soviets."

"Why do you say that?"

Faust relayed the information from Beck. At the end of the telling, Heinz whistled.

"Damn, what the hell is going on?"

"Exactly. Jesus, Joseph," Faust muttered, "my job is supposed to be traffic violations and drunks, not international espionage."

Heinz swallowed hard and rubbed a hand over the stubble on his jaw. "And yet, here we are."

"Yes. And yet, here we are," Herman repeated. "Let's get out of here. Head east. I want to go through Rheinhardt's place quickly. It will be dawn soon, and I don't want to get caught in the light of day breaking and entering."

"What are we looking for?" Joseph cranked the engine, putting the car in gear.

"Any clue as to his whereabouts. We need to find him fast. There's no time to waste. Every hour that passes puts more lives in danger."

Chapter Eight

The Metro Haus apartment building stood six floors high in a middle class neighborhood of the Tiergarten. It was exactly what one would expect a police captain's salary to afford. That appearance ended once Faust and Heinz got inside. After climbing the stairs to the fifth floor, they made their way down the hall to door number 511. It was a corner flat, shaped oddly in a triangular fashion, but it had a terrace that wrapped from one side around to the other. The lock was easy to pick, or at least, it seemed easier after Faust's last effort. He feared he might be getting rather good at being a criminal.

"No lights," he told Heinz, placing his hand over the wall switch as they stepped into the darkness within.

"I know that, Herman." Joseph pulled a small pen light out of his pocket and used it to find their way forward in the living room.

The interior was decorated with expensive furnishings and plush carpets. Nothing inside from the wall hangings to the statuettes cost less than eighteen months' worth of Faust's own pay. It was apparent that Rheinhardt either had a trust fund he hadn't disclosed, or he was involved in illegal enterprises which afforded him the ability to indulge his champagne tastes.

"I'll take the bedrooms. See if you can find anything out here." Faust directed Joseph towards the small library off the living room as he turned to make his own way down the short hall to the back of the flat.

There were two bedrooms. The first one appeared to be a guest room. Faust made quick work of rummaging through the wardrobe and nightstands. Other than a few family photo albums and spare clothing, there was nothing of consequence. The master suite contained a queen-sized four poster bed with royal blue velvet bed curtains. A gold and royal blue duvet covered the bed which was decorated with several matching pillows. The furniture looked antique with brass knobs on the drawers. Herman began with the wardrobe closet, carefully going through each clothing item hanging, checking the pockets. He moved down to the shoes on the shelf, and then started in on the drawers below. Nothing. He moved on to the nightstands on both sides of the bed. He found the usual items one would expect, but nothing of interest. A small desk sat in the corner by the window. If Rheinhardt kept anything of importance in the apartment, it would probably be there.

The oak desk stood upon four carved, curved legs. It had two drawers beneath the surface leaving the rest of the desk open. Inside the first drawer was a small box of stationary, some pens, envelopes, and a pack of batteries. The second drawer was locked. Faust tugged on it, and then pulled out his handy lock picking tools. He found the smallest pick in the group and inserted it into the keyhole. After jimmying it around, it gave with a click. He slid the drawer open and this time, his effort was rewarded. A red, leather-bound personal journal occupied the small space. He lifted it out and opened it. After the first two pages, Herman knew he'd found incriminating evidence that implicated his captain as a traitor. The sinking feeling in his gut made him swallow hard. He skipped ahead to the current week finding the last two entries. He tilted the pages toward the moonlight coming in through the window to better read the words. In Rheinhardt's familiar scrawl was information detailing a public event scheduled earlier in the day that had made the news. Faust recalled hearing a bit of the broadcast while at the hospital. The American ambassador, Peter Holmstead, and his family had attended a ceremony honoring both German and U.S. troops for the holidays. This wasn't unusual or alarming, until he turned the page. Tucked into the binding was a newspaper clipping from the local Berlin Zeitung dated two days ago. The author had interviewed the American ambassador for the piece. Highlighted in bright yellow was Holmstead's own words. "We're looking forward to spending the week with my wife's family back home in D.C. for the holidays. We'll attend the ceremony on Wednesday, and then leave Thursday afternoon. It will be good to see everyone."

Written under the current date was a time and place; 1300 hours, U.S. Embassy. It was circled in red.

"Anything?" Joseph poked his head into the room.

"Yes. Everything." Faust stood, pocketing the journal. It was proof, and he'd need it to convince the authorities of the danger ahead. He'd figure out later how to explain how it came into his possession.

"What do you mean?" Heinz stepped into the room.

"It means I know where Rheinhardt is going to be in less than twelve hours. We don't have much time, Joseph. He's targeting the American ambassador and his family. We need help. It's time to contact the LKA."

By 0700, Faust had met with Colonel von Friedrich, Major Beck, and the head of the LKA, Lars Muller.

"Gentlemen, I don't think I need to tell you how serious this is," the Colonel stated. He paced the length of the makeshift war room Major Beck had set up inside the hospital room on the fifth floor.

Muller's nostrils flared. "Why the hell didn't you contact my office earlier?" He nailed Faust with a glare. "What made you think you could keep this to yourself this long?"

Faust squirmed in his seat but straightened his spine. "My apologies, Herr Direktor, but in light of the threat to my family, and the events of the last forty-eight hours, I didn't know who I could trust."

Muller grunted. "Heads are going to roll!" He pointed at a thin, younger man in the corner, the Assistant Direktor, Victor Platz. "You get me Captain Schneider on the line as soon as he reports in to work." The man nodded. The Direktor eyed the Colonel. "How the hell did you get dragged into this, Colonel? You're retired."

"My niece and grandniece are under threat. And you know better, Lars. We never really take off the uniform. I won't apologize. I'm protecting my own. The rest is up to you. I won't interfere in that, but I'm at your disposal should you need me, and so are my men."

Muller raked a hand through his thinning gray hair. "The goddamn CIA," he muttered. "When those two stiffs came to my office last week, all they said was that they had intercepted 'chatter' about a threat surrounding the embassy. We granted permission for them to investigate, but only in direct cooperation with the Landeskriminalamt, not on their own. Goddamned American cowboys!"

"Did you really expect them to be transparent, Lars?" Von Friedrich asked. "You know better than that. Spooks operate in the dark. Always have, always will. They feed you just enough to gain your trust, and then they screw you."

"Yes, but now we have intelligence that they don't." Muller grinned sardonically.

"And you can thank my nephew-in-law for that," the Colonel stated pointedly.

Muller's grin froze, and then receded. He looked at Faust and his partner in crime, Officer Joseph Heinz, sitting quietly at the table. "Yes, it seems I do owe you a thank you, Officer Faust. It doesn't excuse your activities. You've acted with insubordination, conducting an unsanctioned investigation while not even officially on duty."

"I fail to see how that's a crime, Lars," the Colonel interjected. "If it's his own time, he wasn't acting against orders, especially since no such orders were issued."

Muller slapped his hand down on the tabletop. "He still admits to breaking and entering, Colonel, into two separate residences."

"And stole nothing," the old man stated.

"Except this journal," Muller parried, holding up the incriminating item.

"Look, I know it looks bad, and I understand my duties well, but these have been extreme circumstances." Faust stood, unable to take any more of their bickering. "Furthermore, we have a pressing and dangerous situation that needs a plan, fast, or people are going to die, our own as well as the Americans. If we fail, they'll see it as a hostile act of war. And then what?"

Muller sighed. Colonel von Friedrich stood with his hands behind his back, at ease, waiting. It was Major Beck who spoke up.

"It seems time is of the essence. I can have a squadron of twelve men here within the hour at your disposal, Herr Direktor. Just say the word."

"Mercenaries," Victor Platz sneered. "Hardly Germany's finest—"

"Every last one of them was once Germany's finest, Platz." Beck pinned the assistant direktor with an angry glare. "All served the fatherland, and all would lay down their lives even to this day. They are trained better than even your SEK since they have battled all over the world under every condition."

"For money!" Platz spat.

"For justice!" Beck boomed. "We are not your average soldiers for hire. My men serve me, and my standards are high. To imply anything less is an insult to both me, the Colonel, and to Germany."

"Stand down, Victor." Muller held up his hand, effectively silencing his assistant. "Go call Captain Schneider. We'll need official cover for this in the event it all goes south. Get the SEK director on the line too. I'll fill them in." He turned his attention to Beck. "Call your men. I want them to take the lead on this, but you must coordinate with the SEK. Captain Schneider's men will be on standby. I want an all-points bulletin put out on Rheinhardt, but it's surveillance only. No one is to alert or apprehend him. Just notify me. If Rheinhardt does, indeed, show up at the embassy, we'll take him down. Major," he pointed at Beck, "let's get a map on the table of the embassy grounds and surrounding area. I want to set up vantage points. We'll install undercovers at key locations." Muller began laying out a plan. At the end of the hour, he addressed Faust. "You get some rest. Go home or across the hall, but either way, I need you sharp. You got yourself wedged up into this mess, so you're going to ride it out." His eyes bounced to Heinz. "You too. We'll meet back in two hours."

Chapter Nine

Faust left Joseph sprawled across a couch in the lounge. "Need anything?" he asked.

Heinz stuffed two thin hospital pillows under his head and closed his eyes. "No. I'm good." He lay there, reposed.

"Christ, you look positively morbid," Herman mumbled as he turned to leave. His sarcasm was answered by a soft snore.

Herman walked out into the hall, exhaustion evident in each slow step. He was painfully aware that his wife had no knowledge of his after-hours investigating. She didn't even quite know the whole story on why para-military men were guarding the floor where her daughter had been moved. Between himself and her uncle, they'd concocted a semi-truthful explanation about the ongoing threat from those possibly infected. It hadn't taken much to convince Helga that putting Therese in a private room on a floor in the hospital reserved for officials and celebrities would help keep her safe while she rode out her situation. Her uncle explained that he personally knew the hospital administrator and had requested such as a favor, had pulled a few strings on her behalf, and that until the contagion was completely contained, he would feel better knowing that she and Therese were well guarded. The lie worked, and for that small mercy, both he and the Colonel were thankful, but Herman knew Helga would eventually ask questions. She was a sharp-minded woman. The only reason she hadn't done so yet could only be her immediate worry for their child.

He walked to the side of her bed and picked up her small hand. "Papa is here, Liebling. You just keep trying to heal, okay? I'm right here." He looked around for Helga. She was not in the room. Probably stretching her legs in the halls.

The monitor continued to beep in time with the small girl's heart. The only other sound in the room was the respirator providing oxygen through the tube threaded down her throat. Seeing her lying there, unmoving, broke him deep inside. "You don't deserve this. If I'd been more attentive, taken you to the hospital as soon as your Oma told me you'd fallen and hit your head, maybe we could've prevented this. I was tired, not thinking. I'm so sorry, baby." A tear slipped down his cheek. "Please, God," he knelt, still holding her tiny hand in his own as he began to pray, "please, you who can do all things, heal my daughter. She's just a little girl. She means everything to me. She's my reason for getting up every day, the light in my life. Take me instead if you must, but please, help her, and bring her back to us, for me, for her mother."

The monitor beeped, and the respirator sighed, and the quiet inside the room continued. Herman Faust kissed his daughter's hand and stood as he gently placed it at her side. "I'll be right over there, love. You just rest so you can get better." He ambled to the rollaway bed next to the opposite wall and sat down. It felt as uncomfortable as it looked, but it was near Therese, and the pillow still smelled like Helga's perfume. Faust curled up on his side and closed his eyes. Within minutes, he was fast asleep, unaware of the note that fell off the cot and fluttered to the floor.

An hour later, his pager went off, disturbing the silence. Faust's eyes popped open, and he looked immediately to his daughter. She lay as still as before, monitor beeping, and respirator sighing. The shrill sound rippled once again through the room sending a shockwave through his tired body. He reached into his pocket and pulled out the pager. The number flashing in red was not one he recognized. Rising, Herman prepared to leave the room. His foot slid, and as he righted himself, he noticed a slip of paper under his shoe. He bent down to pick it up, and exited the room, stepping across the hall to the payphone on the wall, never once looking at it. He dropped a coin into the slot and dialed. It was a 00372 number. East Germany, area 2. Herman made the call collect.

"This is Herman Faust," he said. The operator repeated his name.

"Herman Faust making a collect call. Will you accept the charges?" she asked.

A deep, gravelly voice chuckled. "Yes, operator. I accept the charge." The line clicked, passing the call through. "Since I'm paying for this call, I'll keep it brief. I told you not to interfere, Officer Faust, and yet, I have been informed otherwise."

Faust recognized the voice. Anger flooded him as he stood, thinking, wondering how this man knew he was investigating. There could be only one answer. There was a traitor among them.

Major Beck stepped out into the hall. Seeing Herman on the phone, he stopped, directing a questioning look his way. Faust thought fast, and then tilted his head, inviting Beck over. He decided in that split second that the Colonel's man was trustworthy. There was no ulterior motive that he could evince since Beck was on the Colonel's payroll, and until yesterday morning, completely unaware and uninvolved in the unfolding drama.

He considered his words carefully. "I'm not sure what it is you're referring to."

The rough voice grunted. "Don't play coy with me, Officer Faust. You're not dealing with a fool. Remember that I warned you. This operation is above your paygrade."

The man's words struck a chord. His patronizing tone, and reference to a paygrade connected the scattered information in his brain. Taking a chance, Faust dropped verbal bait. "And you're not dealing with a fool, either...Colonel-general Davidovich."

Silence stretched painfully across the miles between them, separated by a wall of concrete, barbed wire, and oppressive ideology. Finally, the man laughed, an amused yet angry sound.

"I see. That is neither here nor there, but your bullheaded foolishness will not be allowed to derail our plans. I've worked too hard, planned for a very long time for this. Nothing is going to stop me or my comrades. Your westernized democracy is going to bleed to death, once and for all." Faust held the phone out for Beck to listen. "And since you're determined to stick your nose into my business, I think I'll begin with you. I keep my promises, officer." He hung up.

"Sonofabitch!" Beck cursed.

Herman stood, shocked, holding the now dead receiver in his hand. He glanced down at the paper he held, finally reading it. "Helga! Jesus! She went home!" He dropped the phone, turning to Major Beck.

"I'm on it." He pulled out a two-way radio, calling two of his men. "Stein, Graf, I need you to head over to the Faust residence. Frau Faust is in immediate danger. A threat has just been received. Voigt, Jensen, Weiss and I will remain here to protect the child. Bring Helga Faust here. We're going into lockdown..."

"Roger that, Major. Over and out." Stein replied, signing off.

Beck patted Faust on the shoulder. "You did well. That was a smart move, calling him out. Now we know who we're dealing with."

"Smart? More like stupid. I poked the bear, and now it wants to eat my family."

Beck shook his head. “No, smart. You’ve rattled him, and agitated men make mistakes. He knows you know things, but not, exactly, what things. You understand? Whatever game plan he had, now it must change. He’ll be desperate. I need to inform the Colonel, and Direktor Muller will need an update.”

“Direktor Muller will need an update on what?” Victor Platz came to a stop next to Beck.

Irritation passed behind Beck’s hazel eyes before he turned his attention to the thin man wearing a gray suit. “Something has come up.”

Victor pushed his hands inside his pants pockets trying to appear intimidating. “Then tell me and I’ll relay it to the Direktor.”

Faust felt a queasy feeling in his gut, one he couldn’t quite explain. He cleared his throat, and began to open his mouth, his attention on Major Beck, but Beck spoke first.

“Come with me. I’ll explain inside.” He directed Platz to the room he used to both sleep and hold briefings. “The Colonel should hear this, too, and I don’t want to explain it twice.” He looked over his shoulder at Herman. “Stay with your daughter. I’ll be in shortly.”

Herman paced the short length of Therese's room. His nerves were frazzled, his body ached from lack of sufficient rest, and his mind screamed at him that something was wrong. He knew Beck's men were enroute to retrieve Helga but worry nagged at him. If Davidovich was as organized as Faust believed him to be, he could easily have someone in place ready to carry out the threats to Herman's family. If that was the case, would Beck's men make it in time before something dire happened?

Across the hall, Beck was busy briefing Colonel von Friedrich and Assistant Direktor Platz. That left three guards inside the hospital. Meanwhile, Captain Rheinhardt was still on the loose. Obolensk's plan of attack was still in motion, and biological warfare was imminent. The clock was ticking, counting down, and if they failed to stop the Soviet's weapon, at 1:00 p.m., all hell would break loose, and the fallout would spread before anyone could stop it.

It was just past mid-morning. Lunch would be arriving soon for Beck's men and Helga. Jasper personally delivered every meal ensuring who the food came from. Faust reminded himself to add a bonus to the man's pay on top of Von Friedrich's payment. In Faust's view, the man was truly an angel of mercy during their time of need. He knew

Helga should be safely back inside the fortified hospital wing by then. One less worry. Still, he paced. The sick feeling in the pit of his stomach refused to leave. He needed air.

Herman grabbed his coat, preparing to walk the hallway, and perhaps poke his head out of the emergency exit door that led to the roof. As he stepped out of Therese's room, the elevator dinged announcing someone arriving on the floor. He checked his watch.

"A few minutes early, Jasper." Faust pivoted, changing direction to greet the man and help him carry the bags.

Immediately, he stopped.

Horror gripped him.

Time slowed as his heart rate sped up. A tall man sporting a blond crew cut stepped off the lift. Decked out in black from head to toe, from his leather boots to a long, leather duster coat, he exuded menace. In his hands, he carried an IWI Mini-Uzi. The fact that Faust recognized the Israeli model weapon and knew it could fire over nine-hundred rounds in one minute felt surreal to the moment where alarms were flashing red inside his head and screaming, 'Danger!'

The hallway suddenly felt like the eye of the hurricane before the storm raged.

Faust reached for his sidearm, unlocking the holster, and whipping out his handgun before shouting, "Beck!"

An explosion of sound shattered the silence. The assassin pulled the trigger, and a hail of bullets flew.

Faust dove behind the nurses' station, knocking the doctor and one nurse to the ground as he went down. Major Beck ran out of his room and down the hall, firing at the blond man, catching him off guard, but only for a moment before he turned the nozzle of the Uzi in his direction. The spray of bullets sent chips of plaster flying from the walls, and shards of glass from broken lights became deadly projectiles in an instant. Herman took advantage of the distraction to attract the man's attention away from him. He peered around the corner of the desk and took aim at the assassin's boots. The first shot missed, but the second hit the toe of his left foot.

The assassin grunted, cursing, and with his free hand, pulled out a Glock from inside his coat. He aimed it in Faust's direction, pulling the trigger. He was now fighting on two fronts and winning. He advanced forward, getting closer to Beck, and closer to Therese's room. Beck's mercenaries, Voigt, Jensen, and Weiss joined the fight. Two advanced from near the elevator, and Voigt came from behind Beck who provided cover. The explosion of gunfire continued as Beck and his men battled it out, their handguns versus one assassin with an Uzi that held them at bay. Faust listened for an opening, peeking around again, taking aim, and preparing to shoot. The man was only three feet now from his daughter's room, having pushed Beck and Voigt back while simultaneously holding Jensen and Weiss in their current positions hiding behind medication carts in the hall.

Faust felt his heart beating somewhere in the region of his throat. There was no way he was going to let this killer get to his daughter. He'd die first. Crossing himself, he maneuvered into a squat, getting ready to spring out. "One, two," he whispered, set to go on three.

A shot rang out from behind them. The assassin stiffened, eyes rolling up in his sockets, as his hand contracted, continuing to fire a hail of bullets from the Uzi. His knees gave way and he fell face first onto the hard tile, unmoving, blood pooling around his head. Dead fingers loosened on the trigger and the silence was deafening.

Faust stood cautiously, looking hard right down the hallway beyond Jensen and Weiss who were still hunkered down. Joseph stood alone, gun still raised, a plume of smoke curling out from the tip.

He looked at Herman and dropped his arm down to his side. "Maybe next time you'll keep it down so a man can catch a little shut-eye."

Relief bubbled to the surface and he snorted, half chuckling. Faust wiped beads of sweat from his forehead, coming to a stand. "Christ. Can't sleep through a little gunfire, Joseph? Don't be such a cranky old woman." Inside, emotions threatened to choke him. Herman turned and ran to Therese's room.

She lay as still as he'd left her, monitor beeping, and respirator sighing. Tears blurred his vision as he realized how close he'd just come to losing his daughter. Beneath the terror and the heartache, rage bloomed. He took a deep breath, knowing he needed to hold that emotion in check. Right now, his daughter and wife needed him. He entered the room and closed the door.

In less than an hour, agents from the LKA arrived on scene, securing the hospital perimeter and the ward. The press came out in droves but were kept outside of the police tape as the body of the assassin was carted out the back via the morgue. Rather than utilizing the city coroner's van, the deceased was transported by ambulance, no lights flashing, and no siren blaring. The quiet exit allowed the agents the opportunity to provide a decoy suspect to be walked out through the front door in cuffs and taken by police cruiser to headquarters. Major Beck volunteered Voigt. A jacket was thrown over his head to hide his identity as the communications liaison, at Direktor Muller's order, informed the press that a lone wolf gunman had entered the hospital that morning and began shooting.

"At this time, the motive isn't clear. What we do know is that there were no fatalities, and no injuries. We'll keep you apprised as we find out more, but for now, this is an ongoing investigation." The liaison stood tall, speaking with easy confidence. As he concluded, the journalists began shouting questions, like a nest of hungry magpies begging for worms. He exchanged a brief look with Direktor Muller who gave an almost imperceptible nod. The signal passed between them, and the liaison waved to the reporters before turning to walk away. The press conference was over.

Upstairs, Major Beck filled Faust and Heinz in on the plan.

"We leave in twenty minutes. I have men already getting into position surrounding the embassy. Muller has contacted them. The embassy staff is aware of the threat, and the American CIA have taken over locking it down. No one will get in, and the ambassador won't be coming out, not today. It's up to us to intercept Captain Rheinhardt..." Beck eyed Faust, "by any means necessary."

Herman nodded. He understood. Even if Rheinhardt surrendered, which was highly unlikely, getting within thirty feet of the man would be too dangerous. That was the radius determined by the American scientists.

"What of bystanders? That's a busy street. How will we keep innocent people from becoming infected?" Heinz asked what they were all thinking.

"The local police have been directed by the LKA to make sure the streets are blocked off. As I understand it, they are using a possible gas leak as the cover story. Undercovers should already be arriving on scene to begin the ruse. Having them there early helps alleviate suspicion."

"But Rheinhardt still must make his way there, and depending on how, it could be putting hundreds of lives in danger." Faust sighed. He reached up to rub the back of his neck.

"Perhaps, but as I understand it, the incubation period has not yet expired," Beck looked at his watch, "but you're right. It will reach its full potency by noon."

Heinz touched Faust on the shoulder. "But the Hoffmann women died before her infection reached the point of being airborne, did she not?"

"Yes, she did." Herman glanced up at Beck. "How do we even know Rheinhardt is still alive?"

"We don't. It's entirely possible he's expired already from the ravages of the virus. The Hoffmann woman was weaker, though. She was frail compared to your captain, and it is still within the realm of possibility that he lives and intends to carry out his mission. There's also the fact that Colonel-general Davidovich has gone out of his way to stop you from interfering in his plans. I'd say Obolensk has high confidence that their weapon is still in play. They are timing this to a tee."

"Dammit, you're right." Faust pounded the table with his fist.

A knock on the door interrupted them. Beck swung the door wide. Standing on the other side was Helga flanked by Stein and Graf. Behind her, Jasper stood holding two large bags packed with hot lunches. There was fear and confusion in both their eyes, and cold resolve in the faces of the two mercenaries.

Faust jumped up, running to his wife. "She's okay, Helga. Therese's okay." He held her tight, kissing the top of her head.

Heinz calmly walked around them. "I'll take that. Thank you, Jasper." Jasper nodded, and backing up slowly, left.

Beck took in the room from where he stood. "Everyone eat fast. We move out in thirty minutes." He paused, and eyed Stein and Graf. "I need you both to stay here, guard Helga and her daughter."

If they were disappointed to be left behind, they didn't show it. Instead, they tucked into the hot food set out by Heinz. It was a quiet meal. Everyone was on edge, and there was nothing left to say.

Chapter Ten

Clouds gathered blocking out any hint of sun. The winds shifted from the north, bringing a cold gust. The temperature began to go south, and with all the moisture in the atmosphere, promised snow before dusk. Faust and Heinz sat inside the back of the black van parked just outside of the cordoned perimeter around the embassy. Outside, SEK commandos dressed as gas company technicians concentrated their performance around a manhole surrounded by bright orange cones. They wore Haz-Mat suits, a precaution since they were located inside the danger zone. Vehicular and foot traffic continued around them, taking the detours set up by the police earlier. Only a few gawkers stopped to watch the workers, and only for a few minutes before continuing on their way.

"What time is it?" Faust asked.

Joseph glanced at his watch. "Half noon."

Major Beck sat in the front passenger seat next to Jensen who was behind the wheel. He looked over his shoulder. “Weiss, make sure they have their masks.”

Weiss stood, reaching over Joseph’s head, and extracted three gas masks from the shelf. He handed one to Heinz, one to Faust, and kept the third.

“Take a moment to put them on and adjust the straps. They won’t work if they don’t fit properly.” Beck demonstrated with his own.

“I’m familiar with how a gas mask works, Beck,” Faust grumbled.

“I’m sure you are, but how often have you had to use one so far patrolling the streets of Berlin?” he asked, eyebrow raised.

Heinz chuckled. Herman eyed Beck. “Smartass.”

“Yes, and also right. Do it,” Major Beck commanded.

Faust pulled the rubber straps over his head and worked the mask into place. Weiss stepped forward, tightening the restraints. He bent down, coming at face level with Herman.

“How does that feel?”

“Tight.”

“Can you breathe?” he asked.

“Barely, yes.”

"Good, then it's working." He turned to Heinz, making short work of his adjustments.

The two men sat, faces disguised by the gear making them alien in appearance.

"Now you look like men," Beck chuckled. His laugh was cut short when Jensen elbowed him, pointing out the window.

Near the corner, just beyond the caution tape, a car pulled to a stop. The blue BMW backed haphazardly into a small, lined space next to a handicapped parking spot. The driver stepped out, barely able to stand. He paused, surveying the area with suspicion.

"Faust, is that him?" Beck asked, beckoning Herman forward.

Through the goggles of the gas mask, he watched the man he once respected, once looked up to as an example for what he hoped to become in the future. Rheinhardt, once a robust specimen of law enforcement, now appeared sickly. His pallor had taken on a yellowish hue. His cheeks and eyes sunk into his face, and as the man lifted his hand to wipe his forehead, it was apparent he was fevered as well. "Yes, that's him, or what's left," Faust confirmed.

The two-way radio in Beck's hand came alive. "Suspect at nine o'clock from our position," came Direktor Muller's voice. Muller was in the back of the faux gas company work truck. "It looks like he's in the full flush of fever, gentlemen. We need to act fast but wait for my signal. Rheinhardt needs to be inside the perimeter. We can't risk him getting out."

Faust watched as Heinz peered around him to get a better look. They both knew from the breakdown provided by the American scientists that once the fever set in, the contagion was fully matured. Even in non-life-threatening viruses, fever indicated that the carrier was highly contagious. When the body temperature rises, it's a sign that the immune system is working overtime to fight off the infection. Being an amazing machine in its own right, the body usually wins this fight, but in Rheinhardt's case, thanks to the biological engineering of Solomon Hoffmann under the thumb of Obolensk, his body would not heal, and he knew it. He'd willingly become infected knowing he would die, and worse, he disgraced himself and his uniform by volunteering for this suicide mission.

It caused Faust's blood to boil that the captain sought to kill so many innocent people by unleashing the deadly pathogen. It was an act of war on the American Embassy, the target chosen by Colonel-general Davidovich, a stealth attack designed to reach far beyond Ambassador Holmstead and his family. The scope of their mission would affect millions of West Germans, anyone on the airplane which could spread to multiple countries, and Americans, none of whom would know what hit them, would never be able to pinpoint the origin. This was ground zero.

"He's coming in," Jensen whispered.

They all watched as Rheinhardt, ignoring the caution tape, slipped under, and began making his way toward the front gate of the embassy. He pulled a Yankees baseball cap out of his coat pocket, pulling it down on his head.

"What is he doing?" Heinz asked, confused by the gesture.

"He's trying to appear American," Faust answered. He looked over at Joseph. "Think about it, how else would he get passed the gate guards? He plans to pass himself off as a sick American in need of help. Had we not forewarned them; it would most likely have worked. If nothing else, he would infect the guards simply by proximity."

"Jesus Christ," Heinz muttered.

Rheinhardt was nearly parallel to the police in HazMat suits pretending to work from the manhole in the center of the street. He cast a sidelong glance in their direction, and when they ignored him, he stumbled forth. His gate wobbled as he struggled to remain upright. He looked like he would collapse any minute.

"Gentlemen, get ready," came the word on the radio.

Weiss, Faust, and Heinz moved to the back of the van where Weiss quietly opened the door. The three men slipped out, taking up position from behind, remaining out of sight. Beck and Jensen had their hands on their door handles, ready to jump out. All around the perimeter, undercovers readied themselves, masks on, guns in hand.

Rheinhardt stopped. From their vantage point, Faust watched as the captain reached into his pocket and pulled out a pager. As he stared at it, his expression darkened. He looked up and around, first at the gates of the embassy, and then at the men surrounding the manhole. Panic flashed in his sunken eyes as they continued to cast around wildly, landing on the work truck first, then two men on the north corner just beyond the caution tape, and another on the west side standing at a payphone, noticing them for the first time. He looked up to the tops of the buildings around the square sighting the sharp shooters. Again, he turned to the embassy gates, seeming to hesitate, and then pivoted and ran back towards the car, and to the crowd at the south end.

He would infect them all!

Without thought, Faust rushed out, putting himself between Rheinhardt and the crowd. He took aim at the man and shouted, "Freeze, Captain!"

Rheinhardt stopped, panting as he swayed on his feet. He squinted at Herman. "Who are you?"

With twenty feet between them, Herman spoke. "It's Faust."

Rheinhardt blinked, and then began to laugh. "Herman?" he choked out before falling into a coughing fit. "How undignified. Here I am, a world-class officer and Soviet agent carrying out a mission that will make me legendary, and the best the west can send is my own patrol officer?" He howled, sounding insane. "That's rich!"

"I'm not the only one here, Captain, as you've already noticed. I just happen to be caught up in your treason. Did you know they came after my daughter? My three-year-old child, Goddamn you!"

Behind Rheinhardt, Beck, Jensen, and the rest of the agents closed in, tightening the net. Beck signaled Faust to keep him talking.

Rheinhardt smirked. "I'd say I'm sorry, Herman, but really, I'm the harbinger of death as you can see. She will die soon anyhow."

"No, Captain, she won't." Faust stared down the barrel of his gun at Rheinhardt.

"It's too late for heroics, Herman." Rheinhardt glanced down at his wristwatch. "I'm contagious just standing here. The public are not wearing gas masks. The virus is airborne. It's flying out of me with every breath." Rheinhardt grinned, a sickly rictus on his pale, gaunt face.

Herman thought about wife, his daughter, his friends. Their lives were in his hands.

"Then it's time you stopped breathing." Faust hesitated half a second, and then pulled the trigger. The bullet flew as if in slow motion, finding its target, right between Captain Rolf Rheinhardt's surprised eyes. The impact knocked him backwards and he landed on the cold, hard asphalt with a dull thud.

Behind Faust, the crowd broke into a panic, running from the scene. For that, he was grateful. Before him, the HazMat suits ran to the body, covering it immediately with a tarp. A HazMat unit pulled inside the perimeter, and more men wearing white suits jumped out. They worked quickly to roll the body in the tarp, place it inside a body bag, and seal it up. The bag was lifted into a container that resembled a cryogenics chamber and rolled into the truck. The second unit came with flamethrowers to cleanse the street of infected blood. Flames burst forth from the nozzles engulfing the fresh body fluids, sizzling until it burnt to a congealed mess, shrinking away until only ashes remained. The ashes were swept up. The captain's car was impounded by a third hazardous materials unit, and in under half an hour, the area was cleared. The LKA kept the caution tape in place, and local law enforcement were assigned to enforce the ban from the area until notified that it was safe for the public.

Faust stood still, his gun hand now hanging limply at his side. Joseph put an arm around his shoulders and guided him back to the van.

"I want to take this damn mask off," he muttered, reaching for it. Joseph stopped him.

"I know, but you have to keep it on until the medics clear us. We're to go through decontamination for our safety."

"I need to get back to Helga. I need to see my daughter," Faust continued to speak, his shock evident.

"You will. Just breathe, Herman. It's over. The rest will pass quickly, and then we'll go back to the hospital."

Faust nodded, letting Heinz know he'd heard him. He tried to breathe, but his heart was still racing. This was his first kill, and it had been his captain, a man he once admired. He couldn't easily come to grips with that, not now, and maybe not ever. Beck arrived at his side, patting him on the arm.

"Officer Faust." He faced Herman. "You acted bravely. You did what was right, and because of you, millions of lives have been saved today."

Herman nodded. He knew it was expected, but he felt disconnected from the moment.

"Come, let's get you both over to decontamination, and then I'll personally see you back to the hospital. I'm sure you'll want to be with your family at this time."

Faust allowed himself to be led, Beck on his left, and his friend Joseph on his right. Inside the mobile HazMat unit, the men went through a sterilization process while still wearing their masks, and then without. Outside, the alien-looking white suits sprayed the entire perimeter until a low cloud of fog hung suspended above the ground. It would remain for the next hour slowly dissipating in the cold.

"The near freezing temperatures were a help for a change," Muller pointed out as he joined them. "The virus couldn't travel in the cold in the same way it would be able to in the heat. Someone was watching over us. Really, that was a major flaw in their plan. Waiting until spring or summer would have been smarter."

"Don't offer them any ideas," Heinz said. "We stopped them today, but who's to say they won't try again?"

"True." Muller stood, arms raised, as he was blasted by a chemical mist.

"What spooked him?" Faust interjected.

"What?" Muller looked at him.

"Rheinhardt. He was on his way to the embassy gates, and then changed his mind." Faust looked from Muller to Major Beck.

The two men exchanged a glance. "A page. He pulled out a pager from his pocket."

"Someone tipped him off." Heinz stated the obvious.

"Who would know?" Beck asked, looking to Direktor Muller.

"Only our inner circle had any knowledge," he stated.

Heinz and Faust shared a look.

Taking in a steadying breath, Herman spoke. "Then we have a traitor in our midst."

"And the answer is in that pager," Heinz added.

"The body has already been taken." Beck's eyebrows came down. "We need to get hold of that pager quickly. The CIA asked to have their scientists examine the body once we took him down. They're waiting at the facility."

"What facility?" Faust asked.

Beck caught Muller's eye and stopped speaking.

"That is none of your concern, Officer Faust." He spoke with authority, and then immediately softened his tone. "We'll handle it. For now, return to your family, be with them. And I want to speak with you both soon... about your futures." Direktor Muller sent one last look at Major Beck before offering a brief nod and leaving the truck.

Chapter Eleven

Helga leaned heavily upon her husband; her knees suddenly weak. The news was not good. Therese's condition was worsening by the hour, slipping beyond the control of her physician.

"I'm sorry, Helga, Herman," Doctor Nguyen said. She patted Helga's shoulder as it shook, sobs overtaking her. "None of the medications are working anymore, and surgery would be too dangerous in her fragile state. The blood supply to her brain stem is being cut off by the swelling. In an hour or two, she will be clinically brain dead."

Faust sucked in a breath as pain sliced at his heart. He doubled his strength to hold Helga up at his side. Behind him, Joseph reached out, gripping his shoulders, lending his support. When they'd arrived back at the hospital, his daughter was coding. Helga had been sent out into the hallway to give the doctor and nurses room to work on Therese. When she saw Herman step off the elevator, she ran to him, and he'd held her up since.

Forty-five minutes passed in which his daughter's brain functions wavered as her heartrate increased, then crashed before being shocked back into rhythm. Doctor Nguyen tried various injections to bring her back to consciousness, but nothing worked. The x-ray cart had been brought in to get views of her head. It was the best they could do under the circumstances since removing her bed from the room in order to obtain a CAT-Scan downstairs would be impossible. The cranial shots at least showed the doctor what she'd feared most; Therese's brain had swelled again. With nowhere for it to go inside her tiny skull, it was cutting off bloodflow to the stem, depriving it of oxygen. Surgery to open a small portion of her skull to alleviate the swelling was too risky while fever raged in her body and sent her into cardiac arrest. There was nothing left to do except pray.

"Oh, God, Herman, what will we do?" Helga wailed.

Her pain added to his own. He shivered, unsure of what to say. His own heart was breaking, and the lump in his throat choked him. The doctor spoke plainly.

"When her brain functions cease on the monitor, she'll be gone. There will be nothing left for us to save. We can keep her body on life support for a time, but eventually, it, too, will give out, possibly sooner than expected after this code. Such episodes weaken the heart muscle, and hers is working very hard right now. It's on autopilot trying to fight off the fever and swelling, even with the medication we've given her. What I'm saying is," she looked them both in the eye for a long moment, "is that a decision will need to be made. I'll be down the hall. Go and sit with her. Call me when you're ready to discuss it."

Herman watched her walk away, and then led Helga inside the room. His daughter lay as before, hooked up to machines and monitors, a tube breathing for her. She looked so small in the large bed.

Helga went to her side, taking her hand. "Darling, mama is here." She kissed her fingers.

"And your old papa too," Herman said, taking up post on the opposite side.

The monitor beeped on, faster than before, erratic. Heinz stood in the doorway watching his dear friends struggling with their pain and grief. "I'll be out here if you need anything. Don't hesitate to call me."

Faust nodded, never looking up.

“Herman, our little girl,” Helga whispered. She caught his eye, pleading for a miracle.

Tears welled up as he replied, “I know.” He put his hand over hers, the one holding Therese’s hand. He’d never felt so powerless. There was nothing he could do to save his child, his light and joy. There was no amount of comfort he could provide for his beautiful wife to protect her from this loss. Herman Faust was in agony. He’d just saved millions of people, but he couldn’t save his own daughter. It wasn’t fair. Herman struggled to take his next breath. All he could do now was hang on to them both, for as long as he could.

For the next two hours, they remained that way, holding their baby girl, smoothing her lovely red curls back from her face, and telling her softly how much they loved her.

At 4:42 that afternoon, Therese Faust’s brain functions ceased. At 6:02 that evening, she coded, and within twenty minutes, her tired body gave up the fight.

A gut-wrenching sound ripped from Helga’s soul, passing her lips, and chilling Joseph to the bone as he stood outside of the room where his best friend’s daughter had quietly slipped away. Her sobs were that of a wounded animal, a mother mourning her baby. It hurt his soul to hear her cries, but when he glanced inside the room, it was the look on Herman's face that haunted him. His friend stood, holding Helga who wailed into his shirt front. His expression was pure shock, like a man lost. The tears in his blue eyes gathered at the corners, blinding him as he stared at the wall.

Joseph swallowed past the lump in his throat. He didn't know what to do.

Major Beck came up beside him, placing a hand on his shoulder. "Come, let's go get some coffee." He led Joseph away as Colonel von Friedrich stepped around him, entering the room. Helga's mother, Margaret, followed. "Let us allow the family their time to grieve."

Chapter Twelve

The sun was especially bright the morning Herman and Helga Faust buried their only child, a steep contrast to such a sorrowful day. The warmth radiating down upon the snow-covered ground allowed for enough of a thaw to proceed with the somber service. Friends and family stood around the small grave at Wilmersdorf Cemetery as the minister spoke words of comfort. Herman bowed his head, holding Helga close to his side. It was surreal.

Just that morning, Faust had awakened, showered, dressed, and then automatically walked to his daughter's room to get her ready for the day. The empty bed was a cruel reminder that he would never again see her sweet smile or hear her call out for her papa as she ran into his arms for a cuddle. He'd dropped to his knees and cried, forcing himself to be silent lest his grief upset Helga more.

His wife had retreated inside herself, a shell of the beautiful, vivacious woman he'd married. He had no idea how to help her...or himself. They suffered together, yet alone in their pain.

A woman signing a hymn brought him back to the moment. He stared at the tiny white coffin. Inside was their child, their baby. Even though the wooden box was draped with pink and white roses, camellias, and lilies, he knew she was in there, all alone and cold. He could not reconcile the fact that she'd passed with the panic welling up inside of him. His brain told him she was no longer there inside her tiny body, but his heart screamed like a wounded animal that she would not be able to breathe, that she would be frightened to wake inside a dark box buried in the frozen ground.

Faust's sucked in air; his lungs starved of oxygen. Helga hugged him tighter as the minister recited a final blessing, sprinkling holy water over their daughter's coffin as it began to descend into its final resting place. Soft music began somewhere behind them. He glanced around noticing his mother-in-law next to Helga quietly sobbing. Next to her, her brother, the Colonel, stood tall, distinguished in his suit. Across from him, Joseph stood holding hands with Eva, the woman he'd recently begun seeing. She was kind, and he knew Helga liked her. The two had been to their home for many dinners and had joined them on outings. Eva had even remarked on how good Joseph was with children after seeing him playing with Therese. This sparked a conversation between himself and his wife later that night over whether Eva was 'the one.' Helga believed she was. Herman admitted she knew more than he did about relationships, so he bowed to her wisdom, earning good husband points for his acquiescence.

Beyond extended family and friends stood Faust's entire police brethren including Captain Schneider. They were joined by Colonel von Friedrich's men, Major Beck and company. He was surprised to see Direktor Muller and three of the Landeskriminalamt agents also in attendance paying their respects. When Herman's eyes returned once again to the grave, Therese's coffin was no longer in sight, but rested at the bottom of the darkened hole in the ground. It was over. She was gone. His heart went with her.

The minister came to stand before them, offering his condolences, and then, one by one, people approached in a line following suit. For Faust, it seemed to go on forever. He felt numb. Finally, there were no more. Joseph and Eva waited patiently until both Herman and Helga were ready to leave and walked beside them.

Near the car, Direktor Muller approached. "Officer Faust, Frau Faust, on behalf of the Landeskriminalamt, I offer our condolences for your loss." He held Helga's hand respectfully.

"Thank you, Herr Direktor," she replied, her voice hoarse from her tears. A fresh round threatened to overwhelm her.

Eva looked at Joseph, and at his nod, wrapped her arms around Helga, leading her back to the car.

When they were alone, Muller addressed Herman. "No man should have to bury his child. I cannot begin to imagine your pain, Faust. You know, I have three children of my own, all of them in their teens now. They drive me crazy," he paused, "but I am thankful for them every day. And I have you to thank for their continued lives. We all do." He drew in a breath. "I know you don't want to hear this now, but Herman, you're young, both of you," he looked over at Helga getting into the backseat of a car, "and I pray you're blessed once again with children."

"Thank you, Direktor Muller." The response was automatic. Herman couldn't think beyond his pain in that moment.

The direktor sighed.

"On Monday, come by my office." Muller handed him his card.

Herman looked at it. "What for? The case is over."

He handed another to Joseph. "You too." He returned his gaze to Faust. "We have much to discuss beginning with where you go next in your careers. Nine o'clock sharp. Don't be late." He gave a quick nod and turned to leave.

"Wait, Direktor?" Heinz stopped him.

"Yes." Muller turned, hands in his pockets, waiting.

"Did you ever discover the traitor?"

Interest lit Faust's eyes. He looked up from the card in his hand. "Yes, whatever became of that? You were going to investigate Rheinhardt's pager once it was recovered safely from the HazMat medical unit."

Muller's face remained stoic. "It's an ongoing investigation, gentlemen, and you are not cleared for that information. Monday. Don't be late." He turned, walking away, then paused, throwing one last comment over his shoulder. "Oh, and if you know any qualified candidates with integrity, the LKA now has an opening for Assistant Direktor." Muller left.

Faust and Heinz exchanged a long look.

“Christ,” said Joseph, running a hand over his face. “It was Platz? That nasty little shit?”

“Indeed.” Herman chewed the inside of his cheek, thinking. “Well, shall we?” He turned, walking to the car. Joseph fell in step beside him as they joined their better halves for the long ride home.

Sneak Peek

Book I, Exposed: The Education of Sarah Brown

Prologue

Berlin, Germany

Fall, 2013

He was beautiful. Absolutely the embodiment of divine creation with his golden curls, blue eyes, and the promise of perfect cheekbones beneath a touch of what people refer to as lingering baby fat. It wasn't fat, per se, but the roundness of youth on the boy's face that would fade away in another year or so. At fourteen, he was angelic. Striking. One could almost see the bones stretching and growing like a young sapling that would one day be a mighty oak tree. For now, they lacked the musculature of a grown man. The limbs were long and the back straight. His blue eyes sparkled when he laughed and were fringed with thick, dark-blond lashes. His cheeks were painted naturally with two spots of color, and his lips, as they spread across his face with a hearty laugh, were lush and full. Even his teeth were pearly white. Perfection.

The very sight of him took the man's breath away.

The boy was tossing a ball to a young woman with red hair. She was older, a sister. Just as lovely and striking, but not so much as the boy. The man watched as the two played a game of catch in the park. He had come to this park every day in the last two weeks since he first sighted the glorious creature. On the third day, they returned with a Frisbee and a picnic lunch. He followed them that day as he did today. They left, and the man trailed them, walking far enough behind not to be noticed, casually swinging his cane as if enjoying an afternoon stroll.

They lived in an old, faded yellow apartment building with too many units to discover which one was theirs. He waited. Two hours later, she left carrying a black duffel bag over her shoulder. He followed her for four blocks where she took the stairs down to the tube and hopped into a car that took them deep into the industrial center of the city. Tourists didn't frequent this side of Berlin. Here, native Berliners came out to party at the clubs and to indulge themselves in the bars. Then there were the others who blended into the hip party crowd, but slipped down back alley staircases to a world most didn't know existed. That's where she went now without hesitation.

He waited, then followed. The staircase led to a steel door painted black. The logo at eye level was three large letters—XXX—painted red. Above those in bright neon yellow were the words 'Club Sexo.' He went inside and was greeted by a glass-enclosed ticket booth which contained a dark-haired man wearing a leather collar with metal studs and no shirt sitting behind the counter. To the left was a door, but it was closed.

"You have an appointment?" he asked.

"No. No, I don't." The man stood there, looking at the list of club rules hanging on the wall behind the host in the ticket booth.

"You have to have an appointment." Shirtless pointed at the rules behind him. Sure enough, that was rule number one.

"How do I make an appointment?" the man asked.

Shirtless gave an assessing glance to the man in the suit. He noted the man dressed well; seemed distinguished even, with his groomed white goatee and hair accented by still dark eyebrows above cold blue eyes. His accent wasn't quite German; more like Dutch. Still, he looked much like the caliber of men who came and went nightly.

"You go online to this website." He handed him a business card through the dip under the glass where tickets were usually presented. "Pick who you wish to see, whatever your particular thing is. All our dommes have bios that describe their specialties. We take all major credit cards, and you pay up front online before walking through that door. The charge shows up as CX3 LLC to protect your privacy. Once your appointment is made, you'll receive a confirmation email or text, your choice, and you just show up. Oh, and no refunds."

"Thank you." The man took the card and put it in his inside breast pocket. He tipped his hat and left.

He made his way back to the UBahn in the quickly falling temperature and found the tube heading back toward the side of town where he was staying. Once back in his room, he shed his suit jacket and pulled the card out of his pocket. He set down his cap and cane next to the jacket. Sitting on the edge of his bed, he pulled out his mobile and surfed the internet for the website on the card.

The splash page asked him if he was over eighteen and to press 'Continue' to indicate he was, and that he accepted the rules for the site. He chuckled to himself. Beyond the firewall was an 'About Us' section and an icon for 'Our Talent.' He tapped that key. Several images popped up of women in various bondage costumes looking alternately fierce and sexy. He found them amusing. Scrolling through, one image stood out. A red-haired woman in red lace bra and panties wearing thigh high red leather boots.

She had a red leather riding crop in her hands and appeared to be smacking it on her palm suggestively. Mistress Elsa, it said.

He tapped her image, and her bio sprang up. *Mistress Elsa is an experienced Domme in the art of bondage for beginners to professional submissives to include extreme roping. Mistress Elsa will bind you, beat you, and/or humiliate you. Your pain is her pleasure. Make your appointment today.*

The man smiled. He changed screens to NOTES and typed. Message saved, he put the card into his wallet and tossed it onto the bedside table. He thought about the boy and young woman. His thoughts went to dark places. Feeling edgy, he got up and picked up his jacket, swinging it over his shoulders and sliding his arms in.

He grabbed his cane and cap. Walking toward the door, he checked his breast pocket for his room key card. Satisfied it was there, he left.

Out on the street, he turned right and headed toward the tube station. A ten-minute ride south and he was stepping onto the platform. He pulled his coat tighter around him. The night air was cool in September. Up the stairs and onto the street the wind met him head on. This was not a decent side of town. This was a slightly seedier area of

Berlin right on the edge of the best tourist spots. Here prostitutes plied their trade. Women from Eastern Europe ended up trapped in this life after being brought in by sex traffickers. Most were strung out on drugs. They looked dirty, ragged, and pathetic, old before their time and used up. The man walked past these women in their platform heels and short bargain basement skirts as they called out to him.

One block beyond were a few young hustlers. Three of them. One was a tall, lean black boy with a shaved head. His shoulders were broad and his arms muscular. *Not him.* The second one had dark hair and a feminine stance. He smoked a cigarette while talking and gesturing wildly with his hands. *Italian. No good. And too many facial piercings.* The third one was more clean-cut with short blond hair. His jaw was square, and he had a dimple in his chin. He hadn't quite yet filled out. His limbs were slim and well-formed. He wasn't overly tall, either. He looked about seventeen, maybe eighteen. *He would do.*

He walked over and asked the young man for a cigarette. The other two hustlers gave him the once-over, noting the quality cut of his clothing, and looked envious. They waved at their friend and moved off, leaving him alone with the man.

Berlin, Germany

Nighttime

The temperature dropped as soon as the sun went down. Anthony de Luca walked around downtown, trying to capture the nightlife of the city on camera. The images would be part of an article he'd been contracted to write for an online tour guide about Berlin. He was being paid for the job, compensated for his hotel and expenditures, and they promised to promote his guide books. He was famous for unearthing the unusual about any city he photographed along with the normal tourist sites. With that in mind, he found himself on a side of town that wasn't quite the best. Still, it was all part of Berlin.

For fun, he'd photographed a few street walkers trying to lure in some business. They were pretty bold, approaching cars as they slowed down to ogle the local 'talent.'

As he aimed and clicked the shutter, he noticed a distinguished looking man walking quickly out of a back alley with a young blond man behind him. The blond was walking fast and shouting at the man in the cap. He was speaking in rapid German, so Anthony had no idea what he was saying, but he seemed pretty pissed.

The blond reached out and grabbed the gentleman's arm and tugged. That was when Anthony noticed the cane in the older man's other hand. That cane came around and connected with the blond's head. Hard.

Shocked, Anthony aimed his camera again, and began shooting picture after picture. The older man continued to strike the younger one on the head, back, shoulders, and legs just outside the alley. Head bleeding, the blond raised his arms to fend off the blows while trying to hit back. He wasn't strong enough for the older man.

Two men came running, one black and the other white with dark hair, and chased off the older man. Anthony kept shooting.

As he half-walked, half-ran away, the older gentleman looked around him. His eyes landed on Anthony standing across the street with the camera in his hands. The slightly panicked look changed to one of dark anger.

"Shit!" Anthony turned and ran back toward the city center. He didn't wait around to see whether the older man would follow him. He knew he could outrun him.

The man did try to follow, but Anthony was soon swallowed up into the crowd, gone. The man stopped to catch his breath.

He wasn't worried that the blond hustler would report him to the police for not paying for play. He hadn't intended not to pay him, but discovered too late that he'd left his wallet in his room on the bedside table. No other way to deal with that situation since the deed was done, but someone else might report him to the police. Someone else with an expensive camera, who was not a prostitute trying to protect himself. Someone who was most likely legitimate. Someone who now had his image on film committing a crime.

He'd have to leave Germany sooner than he planned. He'd have to leave that night; leave before he could set up a meeting with Mistress Elsa. He sighed.

He hailed a taxi. A quick trip back to his hotel had him packed and off to Tegel within the hour. He had no time to spare. If the man with the camera had reported him to the *Polizei*, his image would be on an all-points bulletin shortly, and he'd be unable to get out of the country and back home. He'd find another way to gain what he most wanted.

Read Exposed Now!

Visit micheleegwynnauthor.com

Also By Michele E. Gwynn

Checkpoint Novels

Exposed: The Education of Sarah Brown (novel)

The Evolution of Elsa Kreiss (novel)

The Redemption of Joseph Heinz (novel)

The Making of Herman Faust (prequel novella)

Green Beret Series

Rescuing Emma (18+)

Loving Leisl

Freeing Fatima

Saving Christmas

Loving Freddie

Saving Major Morgan (A Green Beret Series prequel novella)

The Soldiers of PATCH-COM

Secondhand Soldier (18+)
Second Chance Soldier
Second Breath Soldier
Silent Night Soldier
C'est la Vie Soldier (Coming Soon)

The Harvest Trilogy

Harvest (audiobook available free on my YouTube channel)
Hybrids
Census

Section 5 (A Harvest Trilogy Spinoff)

Stand Alones

Darkest Communion (Paranormal Romance, 18+)
Waiting a Lifetime (Contemporary Romance, Mystical)
Hiring John (Romantic Comedy 18+)

www.ingramcontent.com/pod-product-compliance
Lightning Source LLC
La Vergne TN
LVHW041638060526
838200LV00040B/1619
* 9 7 8 1 0 8 8 1 4 8 4 5 7 *